BETHIA

THE HIGHLAND CLAN BOOK 10

Published by Keira Montclair

Copyright © 2017 by Keira Montclair

Printed in the USA.

Cover Design and Interior Format

© KILLION
GROUP INC.

Bethia

THE HIGHLAND CLAN BOOK TEN

KEIRA MONTCLAIR

Novels by Keira Montclair

☾

THE CLAN GRANT SERIES
#1- RESCUED BY A HIGHLANDER-Alex and Maddie
#2- HEALING A HIGHLANDER'S HEART-Brenna and Quade
#3- LOVE LETTERS FROM LARGS-Brodie and Celestina
#4-JOURNEY TO THE HIGHLANDS-Robbie and Cara-lyn
#5-HIGHLAND SPARKS-Logan and Gwyneth
#6-MY DESPERATE HIGHLANDER-Micheil and Diana
#7-THE BRIGHTEST STAR IN THE HIGHLANDS-Jennie and Aedan
#8- HIGHLAND HARMONY-Avelina and Drew

☾

THE HIGHLAND CLAN
LOKI-Book One
TORRIAN-Book Two
LILY-Book Three
JAKE-Book Four
ASHLYN-Book Five
MOLLY-Book Six
JAMIE AND GRACIE- Book Seven
SORCHA-Book Eight
KYLA-Book Nine
BETHIA-Book Ten

☾

TO THE READER

EACH OF THE NOVELS IN The Highland Clan is a stand-alone novel. However, for the richest experience, I would recommend starting with the first novel: Loki.

You'll see there is an extensive list of characters, ones you will grow to love if you start at the beginning.

The Clan Grant Series is the series in which the parents were introduced.

The series can be read separately, but many characters appear in both.

THE GRANTS AND RAMSAYS IN 1280S

GRANTS

LAIRD ALEXANDER GRANT and wife, MADDIE
John (Jake) and wife, Aline
James (Jamie) and wife, Gracie
Kyla
Connor
Elizabeth
Maeve

BRENNA GRANT and husband, QUADE RAMSAY
Torrian (Quade's son from his first marriage) and wife, Heather—
Nellie and son, Lachlan
Lily (Quade's daughter from his first marriage) and husband,
Kyle—twin daughters, Lise and Liliana
Bethia
Gregor
Jennet

ROBBIE GRANT and wife, CARALYN
Ashlyn (Caralyn's daughter from a previous relationship) and husband, Magnus
Gracie (Caralyn's daughter from a previous relationship) and husband, Jamie
Rodric (Roddy)
Padraig

BRODIE GRANT and wife, CELESTINA
Loki (adopted) and wife, Arabella—sons, Kenzie and Lucas
Braden
Catriona
Alison

JENNIE GRANT and husband, AEDAN CAMERON
Riley
Tara
Brin

RAMSAYS

QUADE RAMSAY and wife, BRENNA GRANT (see above)

LOGAN RAMSAY and wife, GWYNETH
Molly (adopted) and husband, Tormod
Maggie (adopted)
Sorcha
Gavin
Brigid

MICHEIL RAMSAY and wife, DIANA
David
Daniel

AVELINA RAMSAY and DREW MENZIE
Elyse
Tad
Tomag
Maitland

CHAPTER ONE

🔾

Autumn 1280s, Highlands of Scotland

BETHIA RAMSAY SETTLED ON THE straw next to the litter of puppies her half-brother Torrian's dear wolfhound had
given birth to a few days ago. The wee squeals that came from the
furry bundles as they pushed at one another and nuzzled their
mother in search of a teat made her smile. Their mother Bretta
stared at her, a bland expression on her face that spoke of exhaustion. It was a chore taking care of six wee ones, even for a dog.

Bretta was still feeling quite protective of her offspring, so Bethia
did not attempt to take any of them away from her yet. Torrian was
the only person the new mama would allow near her puppies for
a while, and Bethia respected that.

A beastly bellow much like the cry of a wounded animal echoed
across the moors between the forest and Ramsay land. Leaping up
from her spot, Bethia yanked her skirts down before she tore out
of the stables to see what kind of creature had made that sound of
terrible pain.

She stood in the doorway, searching for an animal, but the bellows had come from beyond the curtain wall. Eager to see what
was causing the noise—and, hopefully, to help—she hurried to the
gate. To her surprise, it wasn't an animal, but a man, and he was
running straight toward the guard in the gatehouse.

Her brother and laird, Torrian, raced toward the gate. Though
she hadn't noticed him in her haste, he must have left the keep
just when she'd left the stables. She didn't recognize the man, but
apparently her brother did.

"Donnan, calm down," he said. "Tell me what happened." The guard had opened the gates, and the giant of a man tore right toward her brother.

"My dog. Torrian, my dog, Wynda!" He stopped only because Torrian held out a hand to him.

She heard the voices of more guards, men who'd approached to investigate the sound.

"Daft Donnan again."

"He's getting worse and worse."

"What the hell could be wrong with Daft Donnan? There's no blood on him."

When Bethia turned her head to glare at the guards, she saw her mother, Brenna, hurrying toward them from across the cobblestone courtyard. "Is he hurt, Torrian?" Brenna was the healer of the castle, and although Torrian, her stepson, had mostly taken over from his father as laird, she was still treated with the respect due to the mistress of the Ramsays.

Bethia moved closer because she'd heard the man mention his dog.

"Slower, Donnan," Torrian said. "Slow down, I cannot understand you. What is it?"

The man stood at least a head taller than her brother, who was a tall man, and boasted a full beard the color of chestnuts and matching hair, which had probably not been clipped for years. His brown eyes danced back and forth in a look of fear, the kind that bubbled out of the gut and took control of a person.

"My dog. Someone attacked my dog. She's bleeding. I need Lady Brenna."

As soon as Donnan set eyes on her mother, he hurried over to her. He looked eager enough to grab her, but controlled himself enough to fist his hands at his sides instead. "Please, mistress. Please come save my dog." He bent over at the waist, taking deep breaths for a moment.

Brenna glanced at Torrian, clearly hoping for an explanation— who this man was, what had happened to him, anything.

Torrian said, "This is Donnan. He lives alone in a cottage he built for himself near the falls. I gave him a couple of puppies from my last litter, and he has Morda."

Brenna held her hand out to Bethia. "Donnan, I do recall your name now. My daughter is the best healer for animals. This is Bethia. Mayhap she could come along with me."

The man was so undone, he was incapable of speech, tears misting his eyes as he gazed at Bethia. "Please save my dog. Please?"

His contorted face broke her heart, so she nodded. "I'll see what I can do. Let me fetch my bag."

"I'll do it. I'll get it for you. Where is it?" He started to dash off toward the stables before racing back to stand in front of her. "Where?"

The man's wild temperament would have frightened her if not for her brother's manner. He moved over to set his hand on Donnan's shoulder. "I'll get Bethia's satchel. You wait right here for us. You came on your horse?"

He nodded.

"We'll follow on horseback," Torrian said softly. "Bethia, my mother, and I will all come. Will that suit you?"

He nodded. "My thanks, my thanks." He spun on his heel and ran back to mount his horse outside the gates, never once turning back to check on them, instead sending his horse into a full gallop across the moor. The guards who'd come to assess the situation shook their heads and muttered to one another. Before they could wander away, Kyle, Torrian's second-in-command, came hurrying toward them from the keep.

As soon as Donnan was out of hearing range, Bethia turned to her brother. "Is he truly daft, Torrian? Should we be going?" She didn't try to hide her nervousness about the man she'd agreed to help. "Does he live on our land?"

Torrian glanced at Brenna, who grasped Bethia's hand and said, "He's not daft, dear. Donnan joined the clan four summers ago. He used to be a warrior for your father, but his wife left him for another, so he chose to move away and live alone. Your brother was gracious enough to give him three dogs. He dotes on them."

"He takes verra good care of the dogs. He loves them. Trust me. You'll be pleased to see him with any of his animals." Torrian called out for Kyle to assign ten guards to travel with them.

As they walked to the stables to mount their horses, Bethia's mother continued with her explanation. "I had so hoped Donnan would come back to live with the men, be one of your guards, Torrian, but he's not ready yet."

"He may never be," Torrian said. "He took his wife's betrayal verra hard. He's not been the same."

"He's not likely to find another living out in the wild," Brenna said. The stable boy saddled their horses, and Bethia stroked her horse's velvety muzzle before mounting up like the others had done. While her mother flicked the reins of her horse and led them out through the gates, Bethia hung back until Torrian had assigned the ten guards their positions. Then brother and sister rode together to catch up.

"I would hardly call where Donnan lives out in the wild." Torrian laughed, returning to Brenna's comment. "The man appears unkempt because of his hair and beard, but he's far from bedraggled. He's a step ahead of the rest of us, in my opinion."

"What do you mean?" Bethia asked, riding between him and her mother.

"Donnan is clever and he loves to work with his hands. His pups have better living quarters than my deerhounds, and his house is a marvel to behold. Ask him to show you sometime, Brenna. You'd love his contraptions." Torrian took the lead, glancing over his shoulder as his horse galloped toward the path through the forest.

Bethia felt calmer after hearing her mother and brother discuss Donnan's attributes. If the man would trim his beard or his hair, he might not look so frightening. She giggled, remembering her first thought upon setting eyes on him: that he looked like a giant bear. He was tall and broad-shouldered, though his clothing was so threadbare and loose, she couldn't tell aught about the rest of his build.

They traveled through the forest for a ways until they reached the stream that ran to the loch on their land. A large hut built from logs and stone sat on a hill not far from the water, with a separate building that likely served as a stable for his horse. His home was as impressive as Torrian had indicated—it looked large enough for a family of ten, to her mind. He'd used logs instead of stone and wove a finer thatch for the roof. However strange his circumstances, she decided she'd not pass judgment on a man who possessed this much skill and creativity.

Once they neared his home, Donnan bounded out of the stable, which, upon closer inspection, was large enough for two horses and a pen for the dogs.

"In here, mistress," he motioned to her mother, a frantic expression still on his face.

They all dismounted their horses and tied them to a post in front of his house, another convenience he'd added to his home. Bethia followed her mother inside the stable, gasping when she saw the deerhound that lay on a straw mat, the handle of a dagger sticking out of the side of her belly. Two other dogs paced the area, one baring his teeth at Brenna.

Donnan stepped over to his pets, kneeling in front of them. Two were gray while the one with the knife in her belly had a dark red coat.

"Torrian, red fur?" she asked.

"Aye, Donnan wanted her, so I gave her to him. You don't see many of them, and she's a beauty." Torrian knelt down beside the injured dog. "Isn't that so, Wynda? You're quite a handsome girl." He moved his hand carefully toward the animal to see if she would remember and accept his touch. "Aye, you know my scent." His tone was so calming that Bethia couldn't help but smile at her brother. Torrian had always had a natural way with the dogs—it was one of the things that tied them together. He settled his hand on the animal's neck, doing his best to coax her head down so she would relax for Bethia.

Donnan called the other two dogs out and put them in a pen down the passageway. Then he returned and sat next to the injured dog's head. "I was afraid to take the dagger out. I thought it would hurt her more." He lifted the hound's head and settled it on his lap.

"You did right to wait," Bethia said. "Donnan, do you think you need to wrap her muzzle so she won't bite?"

Donnan's gaze caught hers and the pain in his eyes wrenched her heart. "Nay, she'll not bite you with Torrian and me here with her." He focused his attention on the dog. "Will you, Wynda?"

Wynda gave a soft whimper but closed her eyes, as if signaling that she'd heard and understood his missive. Bethia's heart melted as she watched the animal give her trust to the two tall men at her side.

Her mother left and returned with a cloth. "Here, Bethia. I'll pull the dagger out as carefully as I can, then you can apply pressure with this cloth wherever she's bleeding most."

"Mama, grab my satchel. I'm going to give her something to

make her sleepy. I don't think 'twill take much with Donnan and Torrian here to calm her. But I will probably have to stitch her up."

Donnan nodded. "Put her to sleep, so she'll not awaken until the morrow. I do not wish to watch her in pain."

Bethia assembled what she needed, then knelt next to the large deerhound. She gave Wynda a draught to drink, leaving her hand near the dog's muzzle so she would learn Bethia's scent. After examining the area where the knife sat, she grabbed the cloth and said, "Go ahead, Mama. I don't think her stomach or her intestines were pierced."

Her mother knelt next to her, placed her hand on the handle, and looked at her. "Donnan, keep your hand near Wynda's muzzle. She's tiring already, but we'd best be careful."

"I'll not allow her to hurt either of you. Go ahead. Do what you must."

Her mother gripped the handle and pulled the knife straight out, careful not to twist it at all, and Bethia placed the cloth over the spot where the blood was the heaviest.

"'Tis not pulsating, so 'tis not the big vessel, Bethia." Her mother dropped her head to peer into the wound that was about half the length of her hand.

"Aye, 'tis a good sign." Bethia lifted the cloth to examine the wound, trying to determine where she would need to stitch. "The bleeding is slowing."

"Is she going to die?" Donnan whispered, as if the dog would understand him if he spoke any louder.

Bethia put pressure on the wound and said, "I think she'll live. She'll not be running for a while, but I don't see any evidence of damage to her major parts. I'll sew her up and put a poultice on it. You'll have to do your best to keep her from licking the wound as she mends."

Donnan stared at her, his eyes warm and surprisingly trusting. Something in them drew her attention, though she couldn't figure out why. "I'll do whatever you tell me to do. Just keep her alive."

Bethia set to work with her mother's assistance, which made her task go much quicker. An hour later, she sat back and said, "There. I think that should do it. She may never have a litter of pups, but I think she'll be fine in a fortnight." She applied the poultice, cleaned her hands, and wrapped the dog's belly with linen strips.

"I'll leave you something you can mix with her food so she'll stay sluggish. We don't want her running."

"Whatever you say, my lady."

"Donnan, you may call me Bethia. My mother and Torrian's wife, Heather, are your mistresses, not me."

He nodded, his brown eyes telling her how much he appreciated what she'd done for his dear pet.

"She may not wish to eat, and I'd keep her away from the others tonight so they won't take her bandage off. If they try to lick her wound, they may rip the stitches out. I'll come back on the morrow to see how she's doing."

"You promise? I'd come for you myself, but I don't wish to leave Wynda."

"I promise."

"I'll see that she has an escort on the morrow." Torrian helped Bethia clean up. When she finished, he asked, "Donnan, how did this happen?"

The forlorn man finally stood, setting the sleeping animal's head down on the straw. "We were out hunting and came upon a man on horseback alone. The dogs became unsettled, which is unlike them. I called them back and went to speak to the man, but he pulled the dagger out and threw it, hitting Wynda. Her squeals upset me so, I didn't pay any attention to where he went. The next time I checked, he was gone."

Torrian said, "Strange. Someone you've never seen before?"

"Aye, he was a stranger to me, but I haven't been a warrior for a few years."

Brenna and Torrian exchanged a long glance. After watching them a moment, Bethia moved to the pen to pet the other two dogs, reaching over the door. They both responded to her quickly and eagerly.

Donnan's gaze followed her until he saw how quickly the other dogs accepted her. "My dogs didn't like him. 'Tis rare for them to react as such."

Bethia peered at Torrian and her mother, wondering what they were thinking. And yet…in her gut, she already knew.

The man who'd kidnapped Sorcha, Jennet, and Brigid was still out there somewhere, and they feared he'd returned.

Bearchun, a man who bore an unnatural hatred for the Ram

CHAPTER TWO

ↄ

ONCE HE WAS CONFIDANT WYNDA would live, Donnan fetched an ale from his house and brought it outside, taking a seat on one of two boulders he'd arranged around a larger rock that he used as a table. He ran his hand through his hair before he stroked his beard, something he often did when lost in thought. The laird had taken his leave a few hours ago, along with Lady Brenna and Bethia.

The lass had mesmerized him. She appeared to be of an age to marry, and he couldn't help but wonder whether she was pledged to anyone. Though her warm brown eyes and brown hair matched her mother's looks, it was the lass's gentleness with Wynda that had truly moved him.

Everything he'd endured with his wife had turned him away from the thought of taking another woman into his bed. The pain had changed him in too many ways. But there was no denying Bethia stirred something in him.

Mayhap he simply missed being around other people. Missed touching them. He would be pleased just to hold Bethia close, take in her sweet scent, and run his hands down her soft skin. Mayhap that would be enough.

He finished his ale and took out his bow and arrow, whistling for his other two deerhounds, Murdo and Wika, to follow him. They'd hunt some small game for dinner. He hadn't gone more than a few steps when the sound of horses' hooves caught him. He had his bow ready to shoot before he realized it was Torrian and his uncle Logan followed by ten guards. The laird never rode outside the castle alone.

Logan spoke first, as soon as he was close enough. "Donnan, may we have a word?"

Nodding in response, he returned his bow back to its holder, a case he'd built outside his cottage. Logan and Torrian dismounted, and they gave instructions for the guards to patrol the area.

Torrian asked, "How's Wynda?"

"She's still sleeping. I'll take good care of her. My thanks for bringing Bethia to tend to her. She's quite skilled with animals." He pointed to the boulders and the three of them walked over and sat down. "How can I repay you?"

"We have questions," Torrian said. "I didn't wish to ask them in front of my sister or my stepmother."

Logan said, "Tell me about the intruder."

"As I said, he was a stranger to me. Large man with brown hair. No plaid, just breeches and a tunic. He seemed somewhat familiar, but it has been a while since I trained in the lists."

"Do you recall someone named Bearchun?" Torrian pressed.

He thought for a moment, stroking his beard. "Nay."

"Do you remember Shaw?" the laird asked. "He had a cousin who joined the guards for a short time. Mayhap a year and a half ago."

Logan said, "Think hard, Donnan. You may not have been in the lists, but you've come to the castle for an ale, to visit with the blacksmith. The cousins were inseparable."

"I recall Shaw." He thought again, stroking his beard. "Aye," he finally said, the memory surfacing. "I do recall seeing someone with Shaw on one visit. I remember because he was so foul. He insulted everyone he came across, talked badly of many."

"That would be Bearchun. Miserable son of a bitch," Logan said. "Do you think it could have been him you saw today?"

His face lit up. "Mayhap, but the one I saw today had a wound on his face. Cut around his eye. It was still scabbed over, looked quite nasty."

Torrian peered at Logan. "You think Bearchun could have sustained an injury on Buchan land?"

Logan snorted. "With his mouth? That bastard could have sustained an injury anywhere, but aye, 'twas probably done at Buchan land. He must have fought and run."

Donnan shrugged his shoulders. "'Tis all I can tell you. Except that the dogs were snarling before I noticed him. 'Tis unusual for them to turn so quickly. They must have sensed his foul nature."

"If you see him again, let us know right away?"

"Of course. Torrian, may I ask a question? 'Tis personal."

"Go ahead. You may ask in front of my uncle."

He fidgeted, wondering if it was the right time to ask such a thing, but he found himself speaking nonetheless. "Is your sister married or promised to anyone?"

Torrian quirked his brow but gave a simple answer. "Nay. Are you interested, Donnan?"

"I'll be honest with you. I said I'd never marry again, but your sister..." He trailed off, not sure of how much he wished to admit. The lass had moved him, certainly, but was it because of her compassion and her ability to heal animals or was it something more? Perhaps it would be best for him to keep his thoughts to himself until they became clearer. "I was just curious."

"If you are interested, we could use your help with Bearchun."

He scowled. "What does Bearchun have to do with Bethia?"

Logan said, "Bearchun seeks vengeance on our clan. We've been patrolling for him, but not seriously. Now that he's been spotted on our land, we'll step up our patrols and search groups. He has taken two of my daughters captive before, Donnan, and one of Quade's. I'll not allow that bastard to get near my daughters or my nieces again. Bethia could be next. She's sweet and docile, not a fighter like Molly or Maggie. I'm asking you to help us protect her."

A fury built inside Donnan that he struggled to hide. Though he wasn't yet certain what his feelings toward Bethia meant, the lass had saved his dog, and the sweetness in her had given him something he'd lost long ago. Hope.

He'd die protecting her.

"Aye, I'll help."

☾

When Bethia finished her tub bath, she plaited her long locks in front of the hearth, lost in thought. To her surprise, her mind had wandered to the man who lived in the woods.

Donnan was different, very different. Some of those differences were obvious—he lived alone with his animals, his hair and beard were unclipped, and his mind worked differently than most—but there was something else about him, something that made him stand apart from the other lads in her clan. It was dancing at the edge of her mind...

Her hands fell to her lap as soon as she finished plaiting her hair. Suddenly the thought made itself clear to her.

The thing that felt so different about Donnan was that *he noticed her*. He was a caring, gentle man, and he noticed her.

Unfortunately, when she stood in the middle of the Ramsay great hall among her beautiful sisters and cousins, Bethia often blended in with her surroundings. She could walk the entire hall during a celebration, and no one would look at her twice. Her hair was a plain brown, the same as her eyes, and she was wider in the hip than most, something she hated.

She didn't have the arresting beauty of Maggie and Lily, the glossy hair and curves of Sorcha, or the skills and bravery of Molly. She was just plain Bethia. Lads never looked at her—until today.

Donnan was hardly a lad, but a man of at least twenty and six or twenty and seven summers. He had noticed her, stared at her, and actually gazed into her eyes with an expression of...appreciation that had never been directed toward her before.

She'd seen the way her sire looked at her mother, the way Uncle Logan admired Aunt Gwyneth, and even the scorching glances Cailean directed at Sorcha.

But no one had ever looked at *her* like that.

She'd almost felt special.

It was such an unusual experience that she decided to go speak with her mother about it. She left her chamber and padded down the stairs to her mother's healing chamber, knowing that was where she'd likely be this late in the day. When she opened the door, the woman she looked up to more than any other stood to greet her. She'd been scrubbing her table down again.

"Did you have someone with a large wound, Mama? Lots of blood?"

Her mother smiled at her, setting down the cloth she'd been using to scrub. "Nay, you know I like to clean at the end of the day. Just because. I see you were able to remove all signs of the trial you withstood today. How was your bath?"

"Wonderful. You know I could simmer in it until the last of the warm water goes cold. My hair needed washing, and there was more blood on my clothing than I'd realized. I had to wash up before I climbed in."

As she spoke, she found herself staring at her mother. Brenna Grant Ramsay, sister to the renowned Alex Grant, was one of the great healers in the Highlands. Bethia had always idolized her, but now she found herself assessing her mother in a different way: as a woman.

Her mother shared her coloring—brown hair, brown eyes—yet no one would ever call *her* plain.

Could Bethia be considered pretty, too?

"What's bothering you, daughter?"

She shrugged her shoulders.

"Tell Mama," Brenna pressed. "I can see something bouncing back and forth in that intelligent mind of yours." She washed her cloth out in the soapy bucket of water at her feet before running it across the table one more time.

She chewed on the inside of her cheek before she said, "Do you think I'll ever marry? Will anyone ever want me?"

Her mother dropped the cloth and rushed over to her, cupping her face. "Of course someone will want you. How could you say such a thing?"

She did her best to control the tears that begged to flood her cheeks. "You know I'm not like the others. Sorcha, Maggie, Kyla, Gracie…they are all so beautiful, and I'm plain. I'm twenty, way beyond marrying age, and my weight…"

"Molly and Ashlyn were much older than you when they married. I know 'tis oft customary for a lass to marry at ten and six, but not in my family. And you know how I feel about that other word you used."

"Weight?"

"Aye. Weight has naught to do with your value. Have I not taught you that?"

Her mother had tried to convince her that her figure was fine, but after seeing the way lads looked at the shapelier lasses… "Aye, I remember, Mama."

"You'll find someone."

"But how will I know?"

Her mother sat in a chair and patted the empty chair beside

it. "I can't answer that. But you'll be drawn to one person over any other. The more you get to know him, the more you will be drawn to him, but it may not start out that way. At the beginning, you may be more confused than aught else. But Bethia? 'Tis almost magical when it happens."

"Papa said he loved you from the start."

"Papa was delirious with fever when we met. Why all the questions? Would you like us to invite suitors to a party for you? I'll talk to your papa if you do."

"Do you think anyone would come?" No matter how she tried, she couldn't stop fidgeting with her hands in her lap, playing with threads that weren't really there.

"Of course. Bethia, you are more beautiful than you think— your heart beams out from the inside. Anyone who takes the time to get to know you will fall in love with all you represent: compassion, strength, and intelligence. Some men do fear women with a talented mind, but the man who's right for you will not."

"I hope you're right. I would like to have a family of my own, have my own bairns like Torrian and Heather, and Lily and Kyle. Lachlan and the twins are so cute."

Her mother leaned over to give her a hug. "I'll talk to Papa. See what he thinks. Mayhap he has someone in mind."

"You'll not choose for me, Mama, will you?"

The appalled expression that crossed her mother's face soothed her nerves. "Nay. Never. 'Tis your choice. I made my brothers promise that all the Grant woman could choose their own husbands. I would accept nothing less for my own daughters and any Ramsay lass."

She gave her mother a small nod.

At the same time, she hoped she hadn't just made the worst decision of her life. It horrified her to think they'd hold an event in her honor, and no one would show up.

CHAPTER THREE

ಶ

T HE NEXT MORN, BETHIA WAS in the stables, attaching her
satchel to her horse's saddle for her follow-up visit to Donnan,
when her sire arrived. Her father was the mighty Quade Ramsay,
laird of Clan Ramsay until the weakness and pain in his knees had
forced him to pass the lairdship on to her brother. Torrian and Lily
were his children from his first marriage to Lilias, who had died
shortly after giving birth to Lily.

Bethia had many wonderful memories of her sire's days as laird,
but she also loved the stories about how her parents had met. Her
brother and sister had been so sickly as bairns they'd nearly died
from their affliction. Her sire had taken care of them as best he
could, and summoned healers from all around the land to help
them. Nothing had worked, but then Uncle Logan, her sire's
brother, had kidnapped her mother to help the children.

After learning about the children's condition, Brenna had stayed
on Ramsay land willingly, and to everyone's surprise, she and
Quade had fallen in love. She'd also discovered the cause of the
bairns' illness, although it had taken her a while. And that was how
they'd become a family.

The stories reminded her that her mother and father both had
soft hearts. So did Uncle Logan, even though he masked it with
gruffness. Bethia knew better.

"Are you going to visit Donnan?" her sire asked.

With his brown hair and the Ramsay green eyes, he was still as
handsome as he'd been in his youth. If both of her parents were
beautiful, then why wasn't she…? Maybe she was at least somewhat pretty. She couldn't argue the attractiveness of her parents.

"Aye. I wish to make sure the pup hasn't removed her stitches."

"Pup? According to your mother, she's much bigger than a pup."

"In size she's not a pup, but she still acts like one. Torrian has other business to attend to, though he's ordered the guards to travel with me. Apparently, he's sending more patrols out to look for Bearchun. Would you care to tell me more about that, Papa?"

"Nay, we're just being cautious. We have not discovered aught, so there's naught to discuss. I'd rather talk about you."

"You are not using your cane much. Has Aunt Jennie's concoction truly helped?" She patted her horse, giving the mare a touch of love, something she often did before a ride.

"Aye." He bent his knee back and forth as if testing it. "The ointment has made it easier for me to move, so I've been walking more. Still, I try not to strain it with too much use."

"If you're feeling better, would you like to ride with me?"

Her sire's smile lit up his face. "Actually, I would. I can think of little better than taking a morning ride with my beautiful daughter." He helped Bethia onto her horse before he mounted his own. She watched her sire mount, a good indicator of how he fared. He still had pain, but it was obvious he hadn't exaggerated his improvement for her benefit.

Once they left the stables, she couldn't help but ask her sire a very private question. "Papa, do you truly think I'm beautiful, or do you simply say so because I'm your daughter?"

His shocked expression told her perhaps she should not have asked.

"You are a true beauty in my eyes. You must be because you look exactly like your mother, and she is quite beautiful. Would you not agree?"

She couldn't argue his point, so she smiled and nodded.

"Why do you agree with me so readily?" he prodded.

"Because Mama *is* beautiful."

"Why?"

She thought carefully before she answered. "Because she has a beautiful smile and her eyes sparkle when she laughs. Her hair is always a wee bit messy and she still looks lovely because 'tis thick and glossy."

He quirked his brow at her. "Answer me honestly. Before you declared your mother beautiful, did you once consider her size?

She is quite tall for a lass."

She shook her head and chuckled, realizing his intent. "My thanks, Papa," she murmured.

When they headed out through the gates, the guards Torrian had assigned to accompany her fell in behind them, and Quade motioned for three to lead the way.

"Race me, Papa?" Her sire nodded, his eyes sparkling with pleasure, so she flicked the reins of her horse and sent her into a gallop with a giggle, glancing at her sire over her shoulder.

He always let her win.

How she adored him.

Once they reached Donnan's land, they slowed their horses. The brawny man was carrying Wynda over to the stream to drink, cradling the heavy dog as gently as a mother would a newborn babe. Bethia shook her head, wishing she could hear the words he used on his pet. His focus on Wynda was so complete that he didn't turn around to look at them until after he'd set the dog down.

"Greetings, my laird," he said. Though Quade had passed the lairdship onto his son, he would always be the Ramsay laird in many clan members' eyes. "How does your knee fare?"

Quade brought his horse near the cottage. He would likely stay on it rather than walk on his bad knee. Bethia slid off her horse without waiting for his assistance.

"My apologies, I should have helped you dismount, Bethia," Donnan said in a soft tone. He'd hefted the dog back into his arms and was walking toward them.

"I'm used to it, Donnan. How is the dear one this morn? May I have a look at her?"

"Aye, please." He sat on one of the boulders surrounding the larger, central boulder, stroking the dog's neck as Bethia approached them. Wynda seemed to remember Bethia, for her tail wagged briefly when she patted the dog's head.

"Has she been drinking or eating?"

His head shot up. "Nay, she would not eat."

His worried expression brought a smile to Bethia's face. He was a warm, compassionate man for sure.

"She may not feel hungry just yet—'tis normal after such a wound. I saw her at the stream just now. Did she drink aught?"

"Aye, she drank quite a bit."

"Good. Did she sleep well?"

"Aye." He lifted his gaze to Bethia's.

A subtle heat spread through her as his gaze lingered on her. In the light of day, she could almost imagine what he would look like underneath all that hair, clean shaven and trimmed. In her mind, he almost became handsome. And while she would have expected a man living alone in the wild wouldn't bathe regularly, he smelled wonderful. Being this close to the man unsettled her, but in a good way. He gave her that same feeling again—the feeling of being special.

She was glad she had her back to her sire so he wouldn't notice the flush that had crossed her features.

Forcing herself to focus on her task, Bethia gave her head a little shake and said, "I'll check her stitches under the bandage."

Fortunately, her sire began a conversation with Donnan, asking him about the structure of his cottage and all the work he'd put into his living space.

"Many thanks for allowing me to stay on Ramsay land under your protection, my laird."

"Donnan, you fought verra hard for our clan for years. I'll not forget your dedication. What happened to you would definitely leave a mark on any man. If you ever decide you'd like to return to the guards, just say so. In the meantime, I hope you'll continue to keep your eyes out for the one enemy we still have—Bearchun."

"Aye, I vow to watch for him. If I see him again, I'll go after him. I have a wolf that I'll bring along."

Bethia's eyes widened as she glanced up from Wynda's stiches—all fine—and scanned the area. Her sister Lily had a way with wolves, but it was a rare ability indeed. "A wolf?"

"Aye, she stays in the stable sometimes. I know many fear wolves, but she's quite docile around me. She hunts around here often. In fact, she brought three rabbits back for Wynda last eve, but she wouldn't eat. Wika and Morda enjoyed them. I think she's one of the reasons I've not been bothered more often. She protects my area."

Again, Donnan stared at her. She couldn't help but wonder what her sire had meant about Donnan's past. A man would be changed if his wife left him for another, certainly, but the word 'forever' indicated there was more to his story. The expression on his face told her he'd had much pain in his life.

Her father said, "We're planning a small festival for two days from now. Why not come to the hall and share in our supper? We'll have many meat pies with plenty of ale and tarts for all. I think your pet should be much better by then. Do you not agree, Bethia?"

She decided to retrieve more poultice for the dog's wound. On her way back to her horse, she answered her sire, "Aye, she should be getting around on her own by then, especially with Donnan's fine care." She had not heard of any festival, but she thought it a fine idea for her sire to invite Donnan. He seemed so lonely out here…

Her sire must have thought she was far enough away not to overhear him. "The gathering is for Bethia. We're considering finding a husband who would suit her."

Bethia froze, embarrassed that her father had said such a thing in front of her. It hadn't occurred to her that her parents would have already discussed the matter *and* planned the event, for two days hence. Her cheeks felt hot with shame, but what choice did she have but to forge ahead and pretend she hadn't heard him?

Slinging her satchel over her shoulder, she withdrew the poultice from its depths and returned to the dog. The dog allowed her to apply another thin layer to the wound, which pleased her. All the while she treated the animal, Donnan whispered sweet words to the dog, calming her. He had such a relaxing nature, she wondered if he would consider becoming her assistant.

Then his gaze came back to hers.

Nay, she'd never be able to function around him. If his gaze warmed her this much, what would his embrace do? Would she ever have the luxury of being held in a man's arms?

She cleared her throat and said, "I think I'm finished here. Donnan, you've done a fine job with her. I would add some more of the herbs I gave you to her food, just something to keep her a little sleepy. She's still not ready to chase a deer yet."

"Whatever you say, Bethia."

The way he said her name made it a caress, touching down on her ear and then traveling down her shoulder, to her arm, and all the way to her fingertips. She shivered before she stepped away.

"Would you like to see my cottage?" Donnan asked.

She glanced at her sire, hoping he would grant his permission.

Ever since Torrian had first told her about Donnan's house, she'd imagined seeing the inside for herself. Her father nodded to her and said, "You should see some of Donnan's creations. They are quite unusual. Torrian and I have discussed bringing some of his ideas to our keep. I'll wait for you right here."

She didn't need him to tell her why. He was conserving his strength for later, when he'd need to do more walking.

"You have a verra different roof," she said to Donnan, staring up at the top of the building.

"Aye, 'twas something I thought of with my sire's help. He created a tighter thatch to protect from water. I used his ideas and added a few of my own. Come inside and I'll explain it to you." He ushered her toward his door. A few steps led up to the front door, and the area was covered by a small platform and a roof.

"What is this?" she asked, looking over her head at the wooden beams.

"Och, 'tis my own idea. I hated bringing my soaked clothes inside in the drenching rain, so I built this." He pointed to the nails embedded into the four wooden support beams. "You see, I hang my brat or drenched plaids out here to dry before I step into the front hall of my home. When the rain stops, I can hook one end of my plaid to each beam and the sun will help dry it."

She glanced over her head at her sire, who shrugged his shoulders at her. The small smile on his face told her that he was equally impressed by Donnan's inventions. Where had he come up with such unique ideas?

Once inside, Bethia stood in the middle of the large chamber and stared at all his contraptions, pivoting to take them in. She'd never seen the like… "This is so different. And you have wooden floors and walls."

"Aye. When I was young, my papa used to take me out to his hunting cottage and we'd talk about ways we could improve the structure. We hated how wet the floor always got inside once the snow melted. We often talked about ways of diverting the water out of the house rather than allowing it seep in through the dirt floor."

"You found a solution?"

"Aye, with the help of my sire's ideas. I covered the floor with small stones and built the timber floor above it to keep the dampness out. The logs are better at keeping the cold out than the stone, though I use both. I spent quite a bit of time smoothing the edges over so I wouldn't trip on the uneven wood."

"But the floor is quite level."

He chortled. "I've had plenty of time to work on it."

"Donnan, 'tis amazing." She had never seen the like, and it touched her that he and his father had worked on these inventions together. It reminded her of how she'd learned from her mother. "Does your sire live nearby?"

"Nay." A strange look crossed his face. "Come, I'll show you where I sleep."

They stepped into the next chamber and Bethia found herself looking at the softest bed she'd ever seen. The aroma in the room was wonderful. "What is it?"

"Heather. I make my mattresses from heather and bird feathers, though I place the feathers on the bottom so the quills stay away from me. 'Tis quite soft."

Donnan stood directly behind her and she became infused with a sudden rush of heat. His scent seemed to radiate toward her. He smelled of fresh soap with a touch of pine and heather mixed in; he had to be the cleanest man she'd ever encountered. She turned to stare at him and he stepped in front of her, the heat in his gaze matching that in her body. It caused a most unusual reaction in her. Parts of her tingled that she'd not known existed, and she had the sudden urge to touch Donnan's lips.

Her sire's voice caught them both off-guard, almost as if he knew something had transpired between them. "Bethia, are you ready to leave?"

"Aye, Papa." She hurried out of his chamber and then left through the front door. "My, but he is quite creative," she said. "You know Mama would love to have some of his creations."

Bethia stepped on a log and mounted her horse, only then allowing herself to look back at Donnan. "Take good care of Wynda. If you need aught, please let me know."

He smiled and waved, his gaze latching on to her. The people in the clan could call him daft all they wanted, she knew he was *brilliant*.

But there was more to that man than what he created. There was something about how he looked at her that made him different

than any other lad. And then there was the way he made her feel...
Somehow, she knew her life was about to make an abrupt change.
How she prayed it would be in a good direction.

CHAPTER FOUR

ᕲ

FAR OUT IN THE FOREST, a lone man watched Quade Ramsay and his daughter Bethia. Bearchun rubbed his scar as a grin crossed his face. He would do this right, taking his time to attack at exactly the right moment.

He'd decided he would kidnap the old laird's eldest daughter. He'd spirit her away and make them beg him for her return, especially that bastard Logan Ramsay. Ramsay would be on his knees begging in front of him, and he planned to enjoy every minute of the man's torture. He'd found the perfect hiding place, and they wouldn't dare kill him for fear they'd seal her fate. Of course, they'd never find her anyway.

But stealing Bethia wouldn't be enough.

No, he owed them pain and suffering for all they'd done to him.

Bearchun had almost made it as a Ramsay warrior when wee Jennet had discovered his tendency to faint whenever he saw blood. She'd decided a test was in order, so she'd poured red liquid all over herself on the field, pretending it was blood. Sure enough, he'd fainted dead away.

He'd been doomed ever since. Who wanted a warrior who dropped at the sight of blood?

Logan Ramsay was the first one who'd laughed about wee Jennet's test. True, her sire had yelled at her and taken her off the field—he'd even made her apologize to him—but the damage had been done.

All the while, Logan Ramsay had smirked.

And that wasn't all. It had been a Ramsay warrior who'd almost taken his eye out in the battle at Buchan Castle. Ramsay warriors who'd ruined his aim to make money off Simon de La Porte and mad Glenn of Buchan. They'd ruined everything.

But they would pay. All he had to do was to hire his own warriors to help him see it finished. He'd managed to steal some of Buchans' coin—the bastard was dead and had no need for it anymore—so he could afford to pay his fighters. He'd only need them for a short time. Once he had his revenge, he'd leave this accursed place for good and ride for London. There would be plenty of remaining coin left for him to enjoy his life.

But first, revenge would be his.

❧

The night of the festivities, Bethia sat in her chamber, Sorcha fixing her hair. She'd chosen to wear the golden gown Sorcha had given her a while ago. Her mother had done a final fitting so it complemented her curves perfectly.

Throughout it all, one thought had reverberated in Bethia's mind: would anyone show up? She'd mentioned the festivities to her brother Gregor and cousin Gavin to see if they'd give her any hint about who would be attending, but they'd given her their usual teasing grins—in tandem—and left. The two together had been a bit devilish their entire lives, back to the days when they'd guarded the castle with their wooden swords.

She especially wondered if Donnan would come. Though she was still embarrassed that her sire had asked him to come, she couldn't deny she'd be pleased if he walked through the door.

Sorcha finished and spun her around. "Bethia, you are beautiful. You have the most beautiful smile of anyone." She pinched her cousin. "Now, will you not show me that smile?"

"Do you think so? I wish I looked more like you." Her eyes dropped to the floor as she said a quick prayer that she wouldn't be humiliated tonight. "What if no one comes at all?"

"Do not be ridiculous. Of course many will come. We cannot all be as popular as Lily, but you'll have several suitors. You are beautiful and you are the former laird's daughter."

She sighed. "I do hope you are correct. My thanks for dressing my hair…and for the dress."

"That gold gown looks far better on you than it would have looked on me."

Bethia had been hoping to ask Sorcha a question for a while now, but it was a private matter, and she rarely found her cousin alone. Mayhap this was her chance. Clearing her throat, she forged ahead. "Do you like being married, Sorcha?"

"What? Of course."

"Tell me what it's like." She blushed, hoping her cousin would understand exactly what she'd asked. Being a person who cared for animals, she'd seen plenty of them mating and plenty of births, besides, had even heard Lily talking about the act of love. But she wanted to know more.

"Married life?" Sorcha flounced onto the bed, staring at the rafters for a moment. "Come sit with me, and I'll tell you."

Bethia sat down, hoping not to wrinkle her dress too much. She brought her gaze up to her cousin's hesitantly, almost embarrassed by her question.

"First, I'll say I love Cailean more than I had thought possible." Sorcha thought for a moment, then fell back onto the bed, lying on her back and staring up above. "Part of it is how he makes me feel." She glanced at her cousin before lifting her gaze to the rafters again. "He likes to tease me in a way that lets me know how much he loves me. Och, he's always touching me. I'm not so touchy unless 'tis in the dark, but he's touchy all day, morning, noon, and night." She giggled. "Touchy. 'Tis a great word for Cailean. I know he loves me because he shows me."

"Even when he chases you, like at Aunt Jennie's loch?"

"Aye, 'tis when I know he loves me more than aught. He cannot stay away." She turned her head to look at Bethia, her expression more serious than usual. "You'll find someone. Do not worry."

"And the marital part? Do you like it as much as he does?"

Sorcha waggled her brow at Bethia, then sat up and squeezed her elbow. "Sometimes more."

"You do?" The admission shocked her—never had she considered that a woman might enjoy the act as much as a man, let alone more. "More than Cailean?"

"Aye. Sometimes he goes fast and sometimes slow. When he's slow and spends extra time caressing me, 'tis the way I like it best."

The door opened and her mother stepped inside, Jennet behind her. "What are you two chattering about?" Brenna asked.

Jennet gave them a thoughtful look and said, "My guess is they speak of lads and love. 'Tis the silliness that Sorcha loves most, and now that Bethia's gathering is upon us, she's giving her advice."

Sorcha bounced up and hugged Jennet. "Verra good guess, my sweet."

Jennet was the image of their mother, a healer down to her heart, though she was more serious than Brenna would like. Everyone in the family tried to encourage Jennet to smile more, but it was not her way. If Bethia were to guess, she'd predict Jennet would grow to be a better healer than both her mother and Aunt Jennie, for whom Jennet was named.

Jennet replied, "I know not why you think 'twould be difficult. You are quite predictable, and you've been gigglier than ever since you married Cailean."

Brenna ignored her youngest daughter and focused on Bethia. "Are you ready? I think 'twould be nice if you were in the hall before everyone arrived."

"Aye." She stood in front of her mother for her approval. "How do I look?" She turned around so her mother could check everything.

Her mother kissed her forehead. "You look beautiful, Bethia. I do love that gown on you. Nice choice, Sorcha."

Grinning, Sorcha grabbed Bethia's hand and said, "Come. Let's go together. I'll walk down the steps so you'll not be alone."

Bethia smoothed her skirts and pinched her cheeks before stepping into the passageway to wait for Sorcha. They headed down together, and though Sorcha began to babble, Bethia ignored her, too nervous to listen to all she had to say. Her mother and Jennet followed them.

As they headed down the staircase, she slowed her pace to take in the scene down below. They had indeed arrived before the guests, but her sire and uncle were near the hearth, and they both hurried to greet her. The serving lasses moved around the hall, making sure everything was in place. The door opened and Cailean came in with Gavin and Gregor, a few more lads trailing behind them, so her mother motioned for the serving girls to bring in the food and arrange it on a long table near the doorway.

Her mother had asked Cook to prepare food that could be eaten on the move, so the guests could mingle and talk to one another. The minstrels arrived with a couple of fiddlers, and the musicians took their spot along one side wall. A group of lasses from the cottages outside the bailey filed into the hall, their speculative gazes on Gavin and Gregor. Cailean stepped out from the small crowd and grabbed Sorcha, kissing her neck until Uncle Logan cleared his throat.

"Forgive me, my lord." Cailean let his wife go and gave her father an apologetic look.

Sorcha scowled at her father, but that only caused Logan to emit a low growl at Cailean, who grabbed Sorcha by the hand and led her toward the spread of food that had just been set out on the table.

"Hungry, wife? I sure am."

Bethia was happy for her cousin. It always amused her to watch the banter between Cailean and Uncle Logan. The younger man was taller and probably stronger than her uncle, but he was easily intimidated by him. Even so, she knew Uncle Logan trusted Cailean—she'd noticed that they always rode side by side when they left Ramsay land, and Cailean was often assigned to protect one of her cousins, a duty Logan wouldn't trust to just anyone.

She watched all of her cousins: Sorcha and Cailean, Gavin and Gregor surrounded by three lasses, and Maggie and Lily with the twins near the hearth. Molly was off with Tormod somewhere, and Torrian had gone to see Heather. A half hour passed and Bethia hadn't seen one possible suitor. She wandered over to her sire, wiping her sweaty palms down the front of her skirts.

The door opened and a buzz traveled through the small crowd, though Bethia had no idea why. She turned her head and caught sight of a man with a bouquet of flowers headed her way.

Whispers abounded around her.

"Daft Donnan."

"Look, 'tis daft Donnan here for Bethia."

"Is he the only one?" Giggles followed, but she refused to turn her head to see who'd insulted her. More and more of the clan arrived behind him, but she could not tear her gaze from him as he strode toward her.

Donnan had clearly washed and combed his hair, although he hadn't trimmed anything. He greeted Quade first, nodded and said, "My laird."

Then he turned his attention to Bethia, presenting her the glorious bouquet of autumn flowers in his hand, golds and reds fighting for attention. "For you, Bethia."

"Many thanks, Donnan. They are lovely. Where did you find them all?" She took the flowers and leaned down to take in their sweet aroma.

He blushed. "The dogs helped me track down sweet-smelling flowers today."

"Wynda, too?"

"Nay. She's much better, but she only moves to the stream and back. She relaxed in the sun when it peeked out earlier today for a short time." He stood back, his arms crossed behind his back. "May I escort you to the table for something to eat? Or could I bring you something?"

Since she loved the flowers, she didn't wish for them to die. "I'll find a large vase for the bouquet. I'll be right back. Mayhap you should find yourself something to eat while I'm gone?"

Donnan nodded and did as she'd suggested, so she smiled at her sire and moved toward the kitchens. Along the way, she couldn't help but overhear a few more comments—some nice and some nasty.

"Daft Donnan is the only one who's interested in her, and look at all his hair. He never trims it. Bethia deserves better. She has a heart of gold."

"How embarrassing. She's the laird's daughter, and her suitor looks as though he lives in a cave. Does he?"

"Bethia is so sweet. She deserves someone better. Why has no one else come forward?"

"What an odd one Donnan is. Could you imagine giving your daughter to Donnan? I hope the laird doesn't accept his offer."

"Look at that. Even he's gone already. He took three meat pies and ran."

"Donnan hurried out the front door."

"Poor Bethia."

Her lips quivered as she continued on her way, appalled that some already viewed this gathering—and *her*—as such a failure. Had Donnan thought the same? Why had he left so soon? She vowed not to cry, but as soon as she stepped into the kitchens, she dropped her flowers on a side table and fell onto a stool. Sobs wracked her body.

She'd never be able to show her face in the hall again. Donnan had already left, and he was the only suitor who'd declared his intent. She rushed out the door and down the path toward her mother's garden.

CHAPTER FIVE

ɔ

DONNAN WAS HORRIFIED. HE'D HEARD all the nasty things that had been said about him, and it had so surprised him that he'd grabbed some food and left. He'd almost made it to the gates before realizing what he'd done.

Bethia. He'd left without saying good-bye. Worse, he'd heard a couple of mean-spirited comments about her, too. Lasses could be so cruel to one another. He'd seen her go toward the kitchens, but she'd never returned.

He decided to take a chance and see if she had exited from the back of the keep. Mayhap she'd heard the cruel whispers, too, and had left the hall. If she had run from her own party, he wished to console her. He hadn't intended to embarrass her.

There was no one behind the keep, so he turned around, discouraged by the way he'd handled himself this eve. He was beyond the teasing mannerisms of youth, but he'd never heard the term "Daft Donnan" before. Was that what people thought of him? Stunned to hear such casual rudeness, he'd done the only thing he could think to do—walk away.

He could tell Bethia had a more tender heart, and she was so young besides. Perhaps he should return to the hall.

He rounded the keep and froze, surprised to hear the sound of a lass sobbing. It had to be Bethia, so he set his meat pies in the crevice of a tree and listened again. Following the soft noises, he discovered her on the bench in her mother's garden.

He didn't quite know how to approach her, but he'd be damned if he'd leave her to cry alone. "Bethia? May I join you?"

The poor lass struggled to slow her hitching breath enough to speak, but finally she just nodded her response to him. He sat next to her and she angled her body toward him.

He placed his finger under her chin and lifted her red-rimmed gaze to his. "Lass, do not allow the words of hurtful people to drive you to tears. If you cry, make it for a worthwhile reason."

She swiped at her tears and looked at him with such trust it almost undid him.

"My apologies if you heard the name the others used for me. 'Twas the first time I've heard it. Had I known they thought that of me, I would not have spoiled your gathering. I did not intend to embarrass you." He dropped his hand, waiting to see what her response would be.

"I thank you for coming, because if you hadn't come, there would have…would have…" she hitched again, "would have been no one…" The last word came out in a wail.

Och, if only he could bear the hurt of it for her. Life's disappointments could be heartbreaking, and she was young enough to assume the few who'd treated her so poorly could be trusted more than those who valued her. "Bethia, why would you believe a few rude lasses above those who care about you? You have the most beautiful smile I've ever seen and sparkling eyes to match." He smiled. "That is, when they're not full of tears."

She giggled and he was pleased he could draw that from her. Her laughter was a boon to his soul. Then he did something without thinking. He leaned down and pressed his lips to hers.

He gave her a chaste kiss, not the devouring kind he wished to because she was too innocent. He pulled back to gauge her reaction, and what he saw in her eyes made him return for another. She wanted the kiss as much as he did.

He settled his lips on hers, and his hands on her hips. She jumped at first, but he didn't remove his hands, instead tugging her closer to him so he could wrap his arms around her and kiss her.

Really kiss her.

He teased her lips with his tongue until she parted for him, allowing him inside to taste her sweetness. She tasted as sweet as honey. He moved slowly, afraid he would frighten her, but she tentatively touched her tongue to his and he groaned, pulling her closer.

She joined him in his fury, his need for her almost consuming him, but he forced himself to stop. The beautiful lass had brought many things to the brim, things he hadn't thought about or felt in a long time. He felt *alive* again, something he hadn't experienced in years. All that had happened had torn him apart, and he'd isolated himself from everyone and anything since. He'd feared *feeling* again, but suddenly he relished the thought.

All because of a sweet, innocent lass.

But Bethia was the laird's daughter, and he had gone too far.

He set her away from him and said, "Forgive me. I should not have done that."

To his surprise, she giggled and her fingers moved up to touch her lips. "Please do not apologize. I am verra glad you did."

A lass's voice called to her, so she bolted off the bench. Her cousin Sorcha came flying around the corner, followed by a guard he recognized. Cailean. While he'd kept to himself, he'd come to the castle many times to barter for goods and services from the craftsmen in the bailey, so he recognized many of the Ramsays, especially the men from the laird's family. He'd kept up with some of the events this way.

"Bethia? Bethia? Are you here?"

He moved to stand behind Bethia, and she ran to her cousin, who apparently hadn't noticed them in the dark. While he shouldn't be here alone with her, he wouldn't run and try to hide like a laddie would.

"Bethia? Are you all right?" Sorcha asked.

She laughed and said, "I couldn't be any better. I'll go back with you now."

Cailean looked at him with surprise. "Donnan?"

"I heard her crying, so I came back to see if I could assist. I thought perhaps she'd fallen and hurt herself. She's fine."

Bethia said, "He was just consoling me. I feel much better now."

Sorcha narrowed her gaze—first at him and then at her cousin— but she must have dismissed her suspicions, for she took Bethia's hand and said, "Come. Your sire is searching for you."

Bethia followed her cousin, but she glanced over her shoulder and laughed, her gaze catching his.

Donnan had a new goal in life. He would do anything he could to hear the jingle of her sweet laughter again.

❦

Once she stepped inside the hall, all eyes were on her. She blushed, a huge smile on her face because she'd just experienced a taste of what the rest of the world knew.

She'd been kissed for the first time.

Her father appeared at her side. "Bethia? Where are you coming from? The last I saw you, you were headed to the kitchens."

Her father had an expression on his face she rarely saw—he was near frantic with worry.

"Papa? No need to worry."

Her sire asked, "You're not listening to the young ones in the clan, are you? I've heard some cruel comments."

Her uncle Logan and Aunt Gwyneth joined them. "Just say the name, and I'll teach them to mind their manners," Uncle Logan barked.

"Logan," Aunt Gwyneth said, setting her hand on Bethia's shoulder. "Bethia is quite capable of taking care of herself. If someone bothers her, she'll put a stop to it. Aye, lass?"

Before she could respond, Aunt Gwyneth pulled her away from the men and whispered, "Listen, if you need me to show you how to protect yourself, just let me know. Your father would fall apart if you told him aught. But I'll help you."

Bethia glanced around at the family she adored. They truly loved her. She had so many cousins that she often felt overlooked. "Mayhap someday soon, Aunt Gwyneth. I do travel outside the walls often, though usually I have guards with me."

"Just tell me."

Her mother came up behind her and set her hands on her shoulders. "Come sit by the hearth with me for a moment."

She followed her mother away from the crowd that had formed around the minstrels and the food. "What is it, Mama?"

"I was sure you were about to cry when you went into the kitchens."

She settled in the chair next to her mother. "Aye, I was upset at what some of the lasses were saying about me and Donnan, and how there were no other suitors here, but I'm better now. I know 'tis best for me to stay away from them."

"Sorcha cured them of their rudeness."

She quirked her brow, wanting to ask her how her cousin had accomplished it, but decided she did not wish to focus on that part of the night.

"Donnan left early and you ran into him outside?"

"Aye," she replied, surprised her mother had noticed. She'd never been able to fool her mother before. "He helped me realize that I should celebrate those who care for me and ignore the rest."

"Frankly, I'm glad you haven't had many suitors. Remember how confused Gracie said she was when she had her party? 'Tis better to only have serious, mature suitors. Is Donnan truly interested in you? He has a troubled past, but he's still a good man."

She hoped his kiss meant he was interested, but she wasn't ready to share that with her mother yet. "I'm not sure. He noticed I hurried out the back. He also heard what was said about him." She stared at her hands, hating that people were so shallow they couldn't see beneath the surface. True, his appearance was a bit different, but what other man would tend so lovingly to his dogs? His heart was as large as they came. "Mama, you should see all the creations he has inside his cottage. Papa knows all about it."

Her mother quirked her brow, apparently intrigued. "Hmmm, mayhap I'll ask your father to take me out there to see what he has done. It does sound quite interesting. You enjoyed your time with him?"

"Aye, I did. If no one offers for me, I'll be fine."

"But this came about quickly. Mayhap I made a mistake by holding the event so soon. Had we waited another fortnight, the word would have passed beyond our lands. Mayhap there's a neighboring laird who is in search of a wife. I can ask your sire to check."

"Nay, Mama. Please do not. Look what happened to Gracie when lairds beyond the clan learned of her desire to wed. Had she accepted, she would have spent the rest of her life in a castle far away from home. I do not want that. I would prefer to stay on Ramsay land. Please, Mama."

"Gregor said a couple of other lads asked about you, so Donnan isn't the only one who's interested. Why not forget what happened and see who else is here. Do you wish to mingle again, or are you ready to end it?"

Feeling a bit giddy over the kiss she had shared with Donnan, she said, "I'll mingle. I'd like to see who else has arrived in my absence."

Her mother whispered, "I know you are often displeased with your size, but 'tis what is on the inside that matters most."

"I know, Mama. You've told me many times. I wish all felt the way you do."

"Anyone with a strong character *does* feel the way I do."

Her mother followed her back to the crowd. She could see the concern on her sire's face, so she gave him a wide smile before she entered a group around the food table, sidling up between Gavin and Gregor.

Gavin tipped his head toward a lad who was just joining their group. "Bethia, you remember Bothan, do you not?

"Aye. Greetings to you, Bothan. Are you enjoying the food?"

He blushed and said, "Aye. You are…you look pretty, my lady."

"My thanks." Her gaze took in everything she could about Bothan. He was average in appearance. Brown hair slightly lighter than hers. He had kind eyes and a mass of freckles across his nose and a grin that told her he wasn't as mature as Donnan.

Or as handsome.

Which reminded her of something she needed to do. She excused herself and rushed back to the kitchens to retrieve the flowers Donnan had given her. When she arrived, she was pleased to see someone had already arranged them in water. A pair of warm gray eyes popped into her mind.

She carried the flowers back to the hall and set them on a table, admiring them again. What a kind gesture it had been. Then she squared her shoulders and headed back into the thick of the crowd to mingle, promising herself she would not compare each lad with Donnan.

A sigh escaped her lips. If she did, they were all doomed.

☾

Bearchun almost fell out of the tree he was perched in to observe the festivities. Overflowing with happiness, he had to force himself to keep from shouting. The night couldn't have been more perfect. Sweet Bethia was kissing lads already. What a surprise he had for his new partner.

The lass was growing up. This fit perfectly into his plan. There would be even more ways they could use her.

He threw his arms up in the air and almost knocked himself out of the tree.

The possibilities he had for revenge were now endless.

CHAPTER SIX

ᗭ

TWO DAYS LATER, DONNAN TRAIPSED over to the apple tree not far from his property one last time. He'd already carried two large sacks into the cold storage he'd built beneath the ground. There was only enough ripe fruit for one more bagful. He hoped the tree would continue to produce before the first heavy frost settled in.

He moved slowly, turning around to check on his dear friend, Wynda, who continued to improve each day. Today he'd noticed her tail wagging on several occasions, a sign he took to mean that the worst was over for her.

He knew he was too committed to his animals, but they soothed his loneliness and helped fill the hole in his life.

But Bethia called this new life he'd forged for himself into question.

The lass haunted his dreams and occupied his every thought.

It was wrong; he knew that. She was too young, too innocent—too genuine. If she knew where his thoughts carried him, she'd likely be shocked and appalled, so he poured his energy and focus into physical labor.

A sudden scream rent the air. Donnan dropped his sack and raced toward the sound, surprised to hear Bethia's voice yell. "Nay, do not kill him."

As soon as he broke through the cover of trees, he saw the problem. "Wolf!" Donnan bellowed, calling his unusual friend back. Wolf was not actually his pet since she did not sleep nearby, but he'd met up with the huge beast often enough to consider her his friend.

Not looking friendly at the moment, she stood at the edge of Donnan's property with her teeth bared in a ferocious snarl. Donnan came up behind her, dropping his voice to indicate he was not a threat. "Wolf, 'tis Bethia. Stand down." He petted the animal's head and the unusual beast sat, her gaze still focused on Bethia and her escorts. "Wolf, you'll not threaten or harm her ever."

The animal met his gaze, and he felt an understanding pass between them.

"My thanks," Bethia whispered. "She's a beauty."

While others feared the animal on instinct, Bethia seemed to genuinely admire the creature. There were not many who loved animals as much as he did, but it was clearly something he and Bethia shared.

He made his way to her horse, reaching up to help her dismount, then grabbed her satchel for her. Her gaze stayed on Wolf, which pleased him because it gave him the chance to stare at her beauty up close, something he hadn't had the chance to do before today.

Once she had dismounted, she turned to her guards and said, "Please check the periphery. Donnan has control of the wolf."

The guards departed, their gazes darting to the wolf before they left to follow her instructions.

Bethia peered up at him, her tentative smile filling him with heat. He averted his gaze, fearing the consequences if he did not. The lass had a profound effect on him that he struggled to understand.

"Tell me more about the wolf." She didn't move, waiting for the animal to indicate her acceptance of the new stranger.

Donnan shrugged his shoulders. "She visits me on occasion. I've not had any trouble with her. It took her two moons before she would come close enough to allow my touch. Now she comes twice a sennight for a bit of affection from me and my dogs. It took me a while to get used to her, and her to me."

"Strange that she never sensed your fear. Will she allow me to pet her?" Bethia assessed the animal, her eyes alight with excitement.

"Allow her to come to you. The reason she never sensed my fear is that I was never afraid of her." He moved another step closer to Bethia, letting the animal know that he accepted her.

"Never? My sister Lily is special with animals, too. She has two pet wolves that come and go. I thought she was the only one who had that talent. She named her wolves. Have you named her yet?"

Donnan quirked his brow at her. He'd never considered naming the wolf, probably because he didn't consider the animal his. "I'll give you that pleasure. You have special talents of your own, Bethia. Do not discount them. Come, I'll find Wynda. I assume 'tis why you're here. If Wolf wishes to make your acquaintance, she'll follow us." He led her back through the trees to his property, placing his hand on the small of her back to make sure she walked ahead of him.

"Shewolf will not bother my horse? She can be skittish around wolves."

"Is that your thoughtful name for her? Shewolf?"

She laughed, "Nay, but it's what I'll call her until I think of one."

He glanced back over his shoulder, surprised to see the animal was directly behind him. "Nay, I think she's more interested in you than your horse." He chuckled. "And I mean that in a good way."

"As long as I'm not her dinner."

"Never. Your sire allowed you to come alone? I see you have guards, but no close family member to watch over you…or mayhap me." He gave her a side grin, secretly pleased she'd come alone.

"Aye. But only because my uncle has so many patrols out for Bearchun. Torrian is leading one and Kyle another. Molly and Tormod have been sent to Edinburgh to see what they can uncover there. After everything Bearchun has done to our clan, he has become Uncle Logan's nemesis. He will not stop until he finds him." She shuddered, jerking her shoulders up and down. "I do not wish to be a witness to when he finds the lout."

Once they reached the clearing, Wynda, Wika, and Morda hurried to Bethia's side, tails wagging. Apparently, his pets were as enchanted by the lass as he was.

"Greetings, dear ones." She sat on the large boulder, allowing the dogs to surround her.

He watched her as she gave equal attention to each one while Shewolf stood back a safe distance. Donnan fell back to stand beside the wolf and said, "She's worth knowing, Shewolf. After all, she thinks enough of you to want to name you." He tipped his head toward Bethia. "Go ahead."

The beast glanced up at him and slowly made her way closer to Bethia. She held her hand out to the wolf, her fingers folded over, protected from a possible bite. Shewolf sniffed her, then licked her hand before dipping her head in a show of submission. A huge smile stretched Donnan's face, understanding exactly how the animal felt in Bethia's presence. He was not surprised that even the wildest of beasts fell prey to her spell.

The wolf's muzzle nudged Bethia's hand, so she rubbed her behind her ear. "I'll have to find a name for you, dear one, won't I? Or mayhap Shewolf does suit you, after all. 'Tis rather majestic, I think. It reminds us all that you are, in fact, one of the most powerful beasts, does it not?"

The wolf glanced at her, then turned around and took her leave.

"Did I offend her?" she asked with a grimace.

"Nay, 'tis the way she is. She comes and goes at will. Has done for over a year now. I believe she protects us all from whatever is out there, but 'tis a mistake to think a wolf will have the same loyalty or affection for people that a dog has."

Bethia patted her lap and said, "Wynda, come."

Wynda plopped her chin in Bethia's lap, her eyes gazing up at her and her tail wagging vigorously. "She's better, Donnan? Back to normal?"

He knelt down and picked up the Deerhound, careful not to touch her healing wound. He turned Wynda onto her back to give Bethia a good view of the stitches she'd placed. "I feared they were going to fester, but they seem clear today. I've not seen anything green at all."

"Good." She reached into her satchel and pulled out her container of poultice and applied another thin layer, whispering words to Wynda as she worked.

Donnan was lost all over again. Hell, had he ever seen anyone as beautiful, as gentle, as alluring as Bethia Ramsay?

Once she finished putting all her supplies back into her satchel, she folded her hands in her lap and said, "I owe you another thanks for coming to the hall the other evening, and yet another for my bouquet of flowers. They are quite beautiful."

Donnan didn't know what to say other than a quick, "You're welcome." He got up abruptly, made his way to the stream, and filled the bucket he kept there with fresh water so she could wash her hands. When he returned, he sent off the dogs and left the bucket at her feet. He sat on the boulder beside the one where she'd perched and, not wanting her to leave yet, asked her a question that had been on his mind recently. "Bearchun. Tell me what you know of him."

Her entire body tensed while she leaned over to wash her hands in the bucket. "Why do you ask?"

She sat up, her back as straight as an arrow. The mere mention of the man had changed her entire countenance. He wished to kill the bastard with his bare hands.

"I'd like to know more about the man I'm seeking. Your uncle told me verra little about him."

"I don't think he intended for you to search for him, just to be aware. As I said, they have many searches planned for him today and into the night. My uncle will not let up until he finds the man. I don't think 'twould be wise for you to search for him by yourself. He's known to travel with others. Even if you saw him alone before, they think he'll be gathering men to help him. He's already hurt dear Wynda. Do not give him the chance to hurt the other dogs…or *you*. Allow the Ramsay warriors to go after him." Her body seemed to quake with terror, though she did her best to hide it.

This was the same lass who'd trusted a wolf with her life…

"Mayhap not, but I'd like to hear more about him." He took her hand in his, rubbing his thumb across the smooth skin on the back. "I'll not let him reach you here."

She peered up at him and swallowed before she began her tale. "He came into my chamber one night with his cousin Shaw. I awakened and stared at him, not knowing who he was. It was so dark, and I could make no sense of aught until…until he grabbed my wee sister and shoved her in a sack after he forced her to drink a draught. She kicked and screamed and he hit her. The other one did the same to Brigid. Neither my sister nor my cousin recall much after that until the next day. It all happened so quickly, before I could…I didn't know…I was so frightened…"

"Hush, sweet one." He set his finger under her chin and said, "You did naught wrong. 'Twas their fault, not yours."

"I know, but had I screamed that first moment, had I yelled or something, mayhap it would have ended differently. 'Twas all so fast. All I could do was sob."

He hated to ask this question, but he had to. "Did he touch

you?"

"Aye. He tied me up, put something around my mouth to keep me from screaming. The men left as soon as they tied me up. I could do naught. It felt like two days passed before anyone found me, but 'twas probably only an hour. I've never been so frightened."

"Still?"

"Aye." Tears misted her eyes, but she swiped at them. "I cannot disagree with my uncle. Bearchun will not give up. He's fallen in with MacNiven and Buchan and Shaw, all of our enemies. 'Tis why I travel with so many guards and why they continue their pursuit of him."

"Bethia, this I will do for you." She lifted her gaze to his, so trusting, so innocent. "I promise I'll find him and put an end to your fear."

"But..."

"Hush." He leaned over and pressed his lips to hers, molding them to hers for a brief moment to let her know how much he meant it. He ended the kiss and said, "I'll not let him hurt you."

"But why? I'm naught to you."

The words dug into him like knives. Mayhap he'd *like* for her to be something to him. He wasn't ready to say so, but he found himself saying more than he'd planned. "I owe you for saving my dog. There's another reason. I know what fear and pain can do to a person, and I'll not allow it to happen to you."

He held his hand out to her, wanting to change the subject. "Come inside. I didn't get to show you everything when your sire was here. That is, if the guards will allow us." Two guards were on horseback with their backs to the two of them, nervously checking the surroundings of Donnan's property. The rest were searching the periphery instead of staying in one spot.

"My uncle's talk of Bearchun's cunning has worried them. I believe they are more afraid of that blackguard trying to steal me away than aught you would do to me."

He didn't like that sound of that and gave her a questioning look.

"I've traveled with them many times. They believe I'm here to treat your animals. Truthfully, they stopped worrying about my reputation a year or two ago. No one has ever approached me inappropriately. I'm the animal healer. As long as they can see me, they'll be fine."

"But I wish to take you inside. Will they not follow?"

"Nay." She stopped and turned toward one of the guards. "Tonn, I go to the stable to check on the horses."

Tonn waved his hand toward her, never taking his eyes off the trees in the distance. "Aye, my lady."

She shrugged her shoulders. "Do you see what I mean?"

"Aye," Donnan said with a frown, "but I'd like to go teach him a thing or two."

She said, "Nay, then I'll not be allowed inside to see more of your creations, and I so want to see more. You are quite talented."

He scowled, but there was no denying that he wished for her to accompany him inside. She said, "Your home is much larger than any of the Ramsay cottages."

"It seems I cannot stop myself. I keep adding more." He pointed to the steps and the platform outside his door, "Watch your step."

Donnan smiled at her once they were both inside. "I know you were pleased with my main chamber, but I'd like to show you my favorite place in the house. It took me quite a while to complete, but I think you'll like it."

She followed him deeper into the house without question, not even pausing to consider the impropriety of being alone with a man in his home. Her gaze eagerly took in the artful etchings on the walls, the wood carvings in his chairs, and the thick furs pulled back from each window. When she passed through his sleeping chamber, she took a deep breath, inhaling the sweet scent of heather that permeated the chamber from his mattress. Somehow she'd missed another feature of his bedchamber. She grinned and said, "Oh, Donnan." There was a small bed, built low to the ground and piled high with furs, beside the much larger one. It could only be for his dogs. All three could easily sleep there, especially given the way the dogs loved to sleep on top of one another, though she also noticed an even smaller sleeping area in the corner of the chamber.

He followed her gaze and said, "When one of them is unwell. Wynda has been sleeping there."

"But you have the pen outside?"

"'Tis for when I travel. I want them outside protecting my property, but for there to be cover available to them in case of bad weather. There's a small opening they can crawl through into the barn."

The man seemed to have thought of everything.

They moved into the back chamber, and she heard the sound of rushing water, as if a waterfall ran behind one of the walls. She glanced at the number of contraptions lining the chamber, and her face lit up when she noticed the large tub in the center of the chamber. "Oh my." Her smile widened just as he'd hoped it would.

"You like to bathe?"

She tipped her head up to him, her eyes wide as she nodded.

"Good, because I rarely use it."

"Then why did you build it?"

"It keeps me busy. Allow me to explain. I do not like to bathe in tubs but prefer to stand under the waterfall in the summer. One of the reasons I chose this location is because there is a small waterfall directly behind us. My sire and I had often discussed the benefits of building near a water source, and a waterfall seemed perfect. But I could only use the waterfall to wash in the warm months. I wanted to be able to use it even in the depths of winter. After much thought, I found a way to build a channel that hooks under the ledge of the waterfall. Whenever I push this lever, it brings the water into the corner of my chamber." He pointed to a contraption he had built into the wall. There was some sort of wheel attached to it. "In the dead of winter after a heavy snow, this can be verra strong so I had to find a way to slow the force of it."

He stood in the center and showed her every contraption he'd created, explaining its use and the thought he'd put behind it. "If I stand here over the hole in the floor, I can bathe standing up, or I can attach it to this conduit to bring the flow of water into the bathing tub or to fill my buckets for cooking and drinking."

She pointed to a tub at the side of the room. "What is that used for?"

"My back gets tired from washing my clothes in the stream. I dump the buckets of water into it and I have a place to soak or wash my clothes. There's a plug in the bottom with a hole underneath to drain the water out."

She stared at him. "Donnan, you thought of all of this?"

He shrugged his shoulders. "After Glenna left me, I quit the lists and came out here to be alone. I had to do something. These are all things that make my life easier."

They made their way back into the first chamber and Bethia squeezed his hand, her head angled toward the floor as she considered all she'd just seen. What he wished more than anything was to know exactly what went on in that bright mind of hers.

She surprised him. With a look that shot straight to his heart, she whispered, "What really happened to you, Donnan?"

CHAPTER SEVEN

ᕬ

BETHIA CAUGHT THE FLASH OF pain in Donnan's eyes before he covered it. He probably didn't realize she often watched animals for the same reaction, only Donnan's pain had a much deeper root than anything she'd seen before. He pulled his hand away from hers, another indication of his discomfort.

He opened the door and whistled for Wynda to come inside, but left the others out. He settled in a chair at the table and indicated for her to sit opposite him. "What do you mean 'what really happened' to me?" He reached for Wynda, who'd returned to sit at his feet, rubbing her ear.

"I've heard you lost your wife, but I don't think that's all of it. Tell me why you've run from people to animals." She knew her words might be hurtful, but if he understood her at all, he would accept them for what they were—an attempt at assistance.

"Is that what you think I do? Run to animals?"

"It appears you do, but I don't think 'tis the entire story. Why *do* you live alone out here?" She hated to prod him, but she needed to know the truth.

He sighed and ran his fingers through his thick beard. "Mayhap what they say is true. Mayhap I have turned daft." He stared at the ground.

"Donnan? Please don't shut me out." She wanted to know so much more about this brilliant man. Why he lived alone. Why he was so closed off from the rest of the clan, yet so loving with animals. Why he admired *her*.

"Aye, 'tis true I lost my wife to another, but we were already broken. I was broken. 'Twas no surprise to her or to me when she left."

She paused, hoping he would keep talking. She didn't have to wait long.

"I lost more than my wife. We lost our newborn son a few moons before she left."

Bethia's hand flew to her throat. "Donnan, I'm so sorry. I know not what to say." What a tragic event for anyone to endure.

He stood and paced, his head angled toward the floor. "I'm surprised you never heard about our loss."

"Mama just said you'd had a difficult time with your wife. Naught more. What happened?"

"We woke up one morn to find him dead. Your mother came to us, but there was naught she could do." The expression on his face broke her heart. Even his shoulders and the tension in his jaw told her how hard it was for him to even talk about the tragedy that had torn his life apart—the tragedy that had driven him to seek out the life of a loner.

She thought she understood why. Losing another person would be too painful for someone with a heart as soft as Donnan's.

"How long ago?"

"Two and a half years. I tried to move past it, but I've never dealt with such pain. Glenna left me for another man's arms a few moons later. I do not blame her. If I could find a way to ease my pain, I would. But I could not fathom marrying again, putting myself at risk of another loss. I'd not survive it. I'm sorry, Bethia. It was foolish of me to hope otherwise. I like you, but…"

Bethia stared at her hands. How could he ever love someone again after what he'd endured? She would not settle for anything but love. Perhaps she was foolish, but she wished to be in love and have it returned.

A relationship with Donnan would never work. This was the reason he'd been so hesitant around her despite his obvious interest, the reason he'd run out of the great hall as soon as he'd heard someone call him daft Donnan.

He must still be addled by the pain of losing both his wife and son. He had run away because he knew it was the truth.

Now, so did Bethia.

Bethia entered the kitchens to speak with her mother. After leaving Donnan's house the day before, she'd cried almost all the way home. She hadn't been able to discuss Donnan because her heart was broken for him.

Her mother had invited two suitors to a quiet supper so they could get to know Bethia better. The guards, Bothan and Henson, would arrive shortly, but Bethia's mind was on Donnan. She needed to speak with her mother about him.

"Mama?"

"Aye, dear?" Her mother spun around. She wore her favorite gown: a dark green fabric with a golden overskirt. Bethia thought it made her look like the forest in the morning sun.

"May we talk before dinner?"

"Of course." Her mother grabbed her hand and led her into the hall, over to a comfortable spot near the hearth. There were a dozen chairs in an arrangement around the hearth so they could all retire there after the evening meal. "Come, no one is here yet. Is aught wrong?"

"Nay. I just have a question for you." She settled in a chair near her mother. "I visited Donnan to check on Wynda."

"Yesterday?"

"Aye." She played with the folds in her skirt, trying to decide on the best way to ask her mother what she needed. "Donnan told me they lost their infant son. Why do I not recall that? He said 'twas only two and a half years ago."

"Och, child." She kneaded her hands in her lap. "I'm guilty of protecting you."

"Why wouldn't you tell me?"

"Bethia, you did not know Donnan and Glenna back then, so I did not believe it was important for you to know."

"Are you saying you protected me from a tragedy in our clan?"

Her mother squirmed in her chair. "Your heart is too soft. You would have taken this loss verra hard."

Bethia rarely lost her temper with her mother, but she did not like being protected as a child would be. She'd been a lass of seventeen at the time, old enough to understand, and she'd believed she and her mother told each other everything. "Mama. How many other things have you held back to protect me?"

"Naught. Naught that I can think of right away." She shook her head as if denying she'd ever do such a thing. "I didn't see any benefit in sharing it with you."

"The bairn just died? How did he die?"

"I know not. It happens on rare occasion. A bairn is put to sleep and never awakens. One babe I found with its face buried in the blankets. I cannot always explain the ways of our Lord. 'Twas devastating to Donnan. 'Tis why they call him daft. He was sickened by the loss of their son. He was a beautiful bairn." Her mother's eyes glistened with tears. "I do not like to see our clan bury our wee ones."

Bethia leaned forward and wrapped her arms around her mother. "Please promise not to hide aught from me again. I am a woman fully grown."

When Bethia sat back, her mother nodded, wiping away the last of her tears. "Are you interested in Donnan? He is a fine man, a hard worker, a verra gentle soul…"

She shook her head. "Donnan vowed to never marry again. 'Tis good you have two lads coming this eve." She paused, then said, "Wynda is much better. I'll not need to visit him again." The thought pained her more than she would like, but it was for the best. He would never take her to wife.

The door opened and her sire came into the hall, followed by Torrian. Quade sat heavily in the empty chair next to Brenna's, and Lily came down the stairs at about the same time, one bairn on each hip. She set the lassies down near her parents and cleared a path for the two of them, laying down soft plaids to indicate where they should go. The two were now creeping and crawling and getting into everything. "Where's Kyle, Torrian?"

"He'll be here soon. I'll catch one while you catch the other." As if on cue, Lise giggled and scooted down one path while Liliana crawled in the opposite direction. Torrian scooped Lise up and tipped her upside down, causing her to giggle uncontrollably.

"Torrian, Lise is fine, but Liliana will not like that. She'd probably spit on you."

He kissed Lise's cheek and set her down on one of the plaids. The door opened and Kyle ran across the hall to grab Liliana, kissing the bairn's cheeks before he kissed Lily. "Greetings, wife."

Lily fell into a chair. "Finally, someone to help me with these two. They are verra exhausting to chase."

Bethia waved at Lily. "I'll watch Lise. You close your eyes for a few moments."

After the day she'd spent yesterday with Donnan, she couldn't help but look at Lily and wonder how she would cope if she ever lost the twins. She knew Kyle would be completely undone by the loss. After the wee lassies were born, he'd done aught he could to have a quick visit with the bairns during the day, making up excuses like the need for bandages or oatcakes or something. He had long since dropped the pretense. Everyone knew, and accepted, that he stopped back home four or five times a day to visit Lily and the lassies.

The bairns were so sweet, so innocent, so lovable, how would anyone in the clan adjust to their loss? She said a quick prayer that her sister and her husband would never know such pain. Her sire leaned over and scooped Lise up as she did her best to creep past him. Her burst of laughter carried all the way to the rafters. Her father beamed with joy, even when the wee one drooled all over his hand.

Someday she hoped to see the same joy on her sire's face for *her* bairn. Sadness filled her. She'd let herself hope that she might have a real relationship with Donnan, but those hopes had all been dashed. It was foolish, but her heart still reached toward him.

The twins enjoyed their family's full attention for a while until the door opened and Bothan and Henson stepped inside together.

Quade bellowed, "Come in, lads. We're about to eat. Brenna, you remember Bothan and Henson."

Heather came down the stairs with Lachlan and Nellie, greeting her husband fondly before joining the group.

Quade's voice carried over the din. "We can eat. Find a seat at the trestle tables." The warriors would not gather inside the keep tonight. They usually did, but Quade preferred to occasionally have a couple of quiet nights.

Bothan approached Bethia immediately, and said, "Greetings, Bethia." Henson followed directly behind him, echoing his exact words. He was a nice-looking lad, his hair a light brown, almost yellow. It was almost as if the sun tipped the ends every summer. Taller than Bothan, he also had much more confidence than him. Sometimes he was over confident.

"Good eve to you both." Her mother took over and settled

everyone. She seated the lads across from Bethia, placing Torrian between them. Lily sat on one side of her and Heather on the other.

For some reason, she could think of naught to say to either of her suitors. She thought to talk with Heather, but her brother's wife was having a conversation with her mother.

Lily stepped in to help. "Do either of you have any pets at home? You know how wonderful Bethia is with animals."

Bothan shook his head, casting an apologetic glance at Bethia.

Henson replied, "Nay, my mama says animals are too dirty."

"Hmmm…" Lily said. "Yet you're interested in someone who deals with animals every day." Lily was never aught but direct, and Bethia loved her for it. "'Tis a wee bit odd."

"Papa said she'd not be dealing with animals once we marry," Henson said. "A woman's job is to take care of her husband and have bairns." He lifted his chin a notch, as if daring Lily to disagree with him.

Lily peered at Kyle and said, "Husband, when our daughters are of age, please do remind me that their purpose is solely to take care of their husband and have babies. I must remind my mother to stop taking care of the sick in our clan."

Kyle grinned and his eyes danced with merriment when he looked from Henson to Bothan. "Do you not agree, Bothan?"

Bothan cleared his throat and said, "Och, I know naught. She can do whatever she likes as long as she's a good cook."

Torrian rolled his eyes at Bethia, and all she wished to do was laugh. How she loved her brothers and sisters. She decided to come to the two lads' rescue before Lily chewed them up and spat them out with her playful teasing. She had a way about her that tended to catch people unaware until it was too late.

"Bothan, how does your younger sister fare? Did I not hear that my mother treated her for a broken bone? Is she on the mend now?"

Bothan smiled and gave a detailed reply about his family, much to the chagrin of Henson. She caught Torrian's slight nod of approval. Her brother was a master at keeping the peace, and he would likely have dealt with the situation the same way.

The rest of the meal was uneventful, and she'd decided that if she had a preference, it would be for Bothan. The lads had similar coloring, and Henson was arguably handsomer, but Bothan had kinder eyes. He also spoke of his family with love, something she admired.

To her surprise, Henson was the one who strode over to her sire at the end of the meal, requesting that he be allowed to escort Bethia on a stroll out to the gates. Her sire peered at her mother first, then at her, to see if either would object, but he finally nodded. Henson gave a haughty glance to Bothan before moving to her side and holding his arm out for her.

They strolled down the well-lit path toward the gates, but she found her mind wandering to a more mature man with hair everywhere and a big, tender heart. Donnan reminded her of a giant bear at times, but a warm, cuddly bear—one who would protect and cherish anyone lucky enough to find a place in his heart. Henson chattered on about how hard he fought in the lists, not pausing to ask her any questions, so her mind was free to wander.

Which was the reason she responded so slowly when Henson maneuvered her down a dark path. She was caught completely by surprise when he stopped and forced a kiss on her, his hands falling to her bottom and handling her in a way that was most unappealing. She pushed him away and said, "Henson, please take me back."

Henson glared at her and said, "Please, Bethia? Let me feel your breasts first. You know you'll not have many suitors. I'm just here to see what I can..."

"You taste like a frog. You're no catch either, Henson." She shoved at him with all her might and ran down the path leading back toward the keep. He grabbed her shoulder and spun her around, one hand grabbing for her breast, so she did the only thing she could think of at the moment. She made a fist and punched him square in the nose, something she'd never, ever done.

"Ow, you foolish bitch." His hand went to his nose and came away covered with blood. "Look what you did to me." His face lit with a fury that almost frightened her, but she stood her ground, somehow fueled with the fact that she had been kissed by someone who respected her—Donnan. Donnan, who had reminded her that there were plenty of people who valued her, just as she was.

"Tell my sire and my brother, your laird, why you have a bloody nose. See what they think of you then. Go home, Henson, and don't come back."

"I'll tell everyone the truth. You're not agreeable at all."

"Go ahead. I'll tell them the truth. Stay away from me." She twirled her skirts around and ran toward the keep. Bothan was walking down the path in the opposite direction, and she practically bumped into him.

"Bethia? What's wrong? Where is Henson?" The concerned expression on his face did make her feel better, so she took a chance and stopped to speak with him.

"I sent him home. He'll not be seeing me again." She was panting from the exertion of pushing Henson and from being so upset.

Bothan ushered her over to a bench in the courtyard. "Sit, my lady. Henson is an inappropriate lout. I'll go after him if you would like, but I hate to leave you alone."

She willed her breathing to slow down, closing her eyes to calm herself before she spoke. Once she had regained control of herself, she opened her eyes and said, "Many thanks to you, Bothan. I am fine. I'd like to return to the hall." The expression on his face was full of kindness, candor and openness. This wasn't the type of lad who'd insist on getting his own way, no matter whom it hurt.

"Of course." They moved back to the hall in silence, and he held the door for her.

Inside, her family sat gathered around the hearth, and they all turned in unison to greet her.

She announced, "I sent Henson home." She turned back to Bothan and said, "My thanks for your escort, Bothan, but I'm a little tired from the events of the day. I'll see you another day."

He nodded and left.

As soon as the door closed behind him, her shoulders slumped. Her dear sister Lily ran over to her and said in a voice she likely thought no one could overhear, "Henson tasted like boar meat, did he not?"

She burst into gales of laughter and replied, "I thought more like a frog."

Kyle said, "Lily...?"

"Oh, Kyle. 'Twas long before I fell in love with you. You are the only one for me." She grinned and tugged Bethia over to the hearth. Wee Lise sat on the floor clapping her hands with a grin on her face.

The morrow would probably bring another suitor, but Bethia's mind kept returning to one man who was much more mature than the others. To a man who stood out. She vowed to speak to Lily about Donnan.

She'd know exactly what to do.

CHAPTER EIGHT

D ONNAN SPOKE TO EACH OF his dear pets before they departed for a hunting expedition. It had been three days since he'd last seen Bethia, and the lass still occupied his mind all day and half the night. He slept terribly, but he refused to talk to Quade Ramsay about his daughter. She was such a warm, giving soul that she deserved to have bairns of her own. He could not go through such torment again, therefore he needed to stay away from her.

He'd finally made his mind up to do something about his obses-sion. The lass had a genuine fear of Bearchun, so he'd vowed to find him. As the lass had told him, the Ramsays were sending out near constant patrols, but naught had become of it yet. Mayhap it was time for him to take action, allow his dogs to locate the lout's foul scent.

Today he'd begin a search of the land around him for any sign of a reiver or lone guard in the woods. He agreed with Logan Ram-say—the bastard was around somewhere. The wolf had stopped by more often, as if something disturbing was out there.

He'd find the bastard and kill him for his sweet Bethia. He reached into his sporran and pulled out the linen square she'd left behind one day. He hadn't noticed it at the time, but Wynda had brought it to him. He knew it was hers because it carried her sweet scent.

Mayhap it had been foolish of him to save it, but it served as a reminder that there were still good things in life. He tugged it out and brought it to his nose, inhaling lightly. Hellfire, but her scent was sweet. She smelled of pine and flowers.

He reached out to pat Wynda's head. "I know you miss her, Wynda. So do I. But 'twas wrong of me to take advantage of such an innocent lass. The only way I can think to right my wrong is to find the bastard who frightens her."

Her muzzle nudged his hand, as if she was trying to tell him something. "Och, you wish to help me find the bastard? All right, I'll take you along. We'll not go far our first day. You know whom we search for, aye? The man who put that dagger in your belly. We need to find him."

He mounted up and whistled for his dogs to follow him. The deerhounds would not fail him. He hadn't gone far when he noticed Shewolf off to his side, her dark coat glistening under the rare sunshine. The beast appeared to be intent on keeping an eye on them. "You're welcome to assist us, Shewolf. I'll take all the help I can get."

They traveled from ravine to ravine, following paths through the forest, but he found nothing. Late in the afternoon, he caught sight of something in front of a nearby outcropping—a piece of material left behind. It was a small piece of plaid.

Dismounting, he checked the area carefully for any other signs, unsheathing his sword as soon as his boots landed in the dirt. Wika and Morda both sniffed around, finding castoff rabbit bones nearby, but it was Wynda's reaction to the piece of fabric that told him he'd found something. As soon as she caught the scent, she whined and ran in a circle, yipping. He had to sit on a boulder and settle her down before he could do anything else.

Once she was calm, he tucked the scrap of fabric into his sporran and rode hard toward Ramsay land. He knew what he had to do.

As soon as he approached the gates, Kyle Maule called out to him. "Donnan. Problem?"

"I need to see Logan Ramsay and your laird. 'Tis important."

"Bearchun?" Kyle asked immediately, his face tightening.

"I believe so."

Kyle opened the gates for him, ushering him inside, and then disappeared into the keep. A few moments later, he reappeared with Logan Ramsay. "You found him?"

"Nay, but I found a scrap of his clothing. From the way Wynda reacted, I could tell it has his scent on it. Now that I have a way of tracking him, my dogs will find the bastard."

Torrian came up behind Logan and Kyle. "How far out?"

"Southeast of your land. Mayhap he came from Edinburgh. I'm going after him. Came to see if you'd free a couple of guards to travel with me."

Logan's gaze narrowed. "Why you? What is he to you?"

A small frame exited the stables and walked directly toward them. He nodded toward Bethia. "Repayment for saving my dog. I owe Bethia. I don't like what he did to your lasses, and I can see the fear in her eyes every time she hears his name. He also injured Wynda. I have plenty of reasons to seek out the bastard."

Logan took his measure, then turned to Kyle. "Tell the stable lads to saddle my horse. I'm going with him, and we're taking five guards."

Torrian said, "I'm coming, too. Saddle another," he said to his second, the man who would take care of the Ramsay Castle in his absence. His sire would also stay behind.

Bethia continued on toward Donnan, not saying a word even though she was now close enough, carrying herself as regally as any queen. "You're going after Bearchun?" she finally said.

"Aye," Donnan replied. "Might I leave Wynda with you? I think 'twould be too much for her. Morda and Wika will pick up his scent from a piece of cloth I found. Shewolf wishes to travel with us."

The stable boy had emerged with two horses saddled for the ride. The five guards rode up after him. "Shewolf? One of my niece's wolves?"

"Nay. A wolf lives near me in the woods. She likes to follow me, though she keeps her distance. If you're afraid of a wolf, don't come along. She's persistent. There's something out there she doesn't like."

Logan glanced at Torrian. "They don't scare me if they have a master and they aren't in a pack. Does she travel alone?"

"Aye. Never seen another," Donnan said.

"You her master?"

Donnan stroked his beard. "Seems so."

"I want Bearchun. And if she leads me to the rotten bastard, I'll cut his body into pieces and roast them for her dinner."

Donnan glanced at Bethia again. "May I impose on you?"

Her eyes were wide with alarm, but she shook it off. "Of course.

Wynda, come." She turned her hand over to signal for the deer-hound to join her.

The animal glanced up at her owner. "Go with Bethia, Wynda. I'll return for you."

The hound trotted over to Bethia's side and awaited further instructions. Logan said, "Bethia, tell Gwyneth where we've gone. I hope the hounds do their job and find him fast. Tell her there are five guards with us, and that we could not afford to wait."

Torrian said, "And talk to Heather for me. I agree that this cannot wait."

Bethia nodded, glancing over her brother's shoulder at Donnan. He didn't like the fear and concern he saw in her eyes, and he vowed anew to put an end to it.

Logan mounted and turned his horse around, heading toward the lists. "MacAdam," he cried out to Cailean. "Be prepared. I may come back for you." He glanced over his shoulder at Torrian, then Donnan, and said, "Time for some hunting."

❧

It took them two hours to find anything. Morda had tracked the scent, but apparently Bearchun had been moving quickly. They were more than halfway between Edinburgh and Ramsay land when Shewolf joined them.

He could tell from the way the beast held her head that they were close to something. He watched as she crept lower, her ears on alert, pulling closer to Donnan and Morda. As if on cue, all three animals took off in one direction.

Logan yelled, "Archer, keep down." He sent three guards after the dogs.

An arrow sluiced through the sky and caught the wolf in her flank, her cries echoing across the land. Torrian and Logan found protection in the pushes off to the side of their path, dismounting to get out of the archer's line of sight.

Donnan couldn't believe it. Aye, he'd seen where the arrow had come from, but his gut told him Bearchun was in the opposite direction. He headed off toward a copse of trees behind a group of boulders.

"Donnan, get the hell back here. He'll take you out with an arrow."

"Nay, 'tis a ruse. He's up in the trees," he shouted over his shoulder as he rode his horse in that direction. His gaze scanned the area and he slowed his mount. As soon as he heard the sound of footsteps in the trees, he dismounted. The bastard was here; he could almost smell him.

He crept around the group of boulders. The others were headed in the other direction, including his dogs and the now injured wolf, although he had no idea if she still moved.

He came around the boulder, his hand tightly gripped on the hilt of his sword. Sweat dripped down his forehead, but he ignored it. A pair of sweet brown eyes flashed through his mind, driving him to catch the blackguard who'd dared to touch Bethia.

The night was as still as the glassy surface of a loch. An oppressive silence now hung over the area. The only sounds he heard were the cries of the wolf and the hoot of an owl off in the distance. A shadow crossed his vision off to the side, and he spun around only to see a fox running in the opposite direction.

He wiped his forehead again and took two more steps forward, the slight crunch of the leaves beneath his boots giving him away.

A figure jumped out at him from behind a tree, a dagger raised in his right hand, and charged directly at him. He swung his sword, catching the lout in the shoulder, but not before the dagger sliced across his side just below his ribcage.

His attacker turned and ran, mounted the horse he'd hidden in the trees, and took off in the opposite direction of the Ramsay guards.

"Ramsay!" He wished to warn the others that the man was on the run.

He'd seen enough of the man's face to know it was Bearchun, a scar running across his forehead and into his cheek. It had been scabbed before, but now it just looked red and raw. His left hand moved to his side, the warm liquid from his wound dripping over his fingers. He stared at the blood oozing out, the sting from the blade just now registering.

He'd failed her.

"Bethia, forgive me."

He dropped his sword and staggered back toward a large boulder, resting his right hand on top of the rock to steady himself. His gaze searched the area for Logan or Torrian, anyone.

Morda raced toward him. He forced himself to put one foot in front of the other and moved toward his horse, still tied to the tree where he'd left her, his hand still pressed to the wound that was nearly as long as his hand. He untied her reins and started to lead her toward the Ramsay men, his walk more of a lurch.

Off in the distance, another man came out of the bushes and jumped onto his horse, also hidden in the brush, before heading in the same direction as Bearchun. Donnan had almost reached the others before Logan turned around, his gaze noticing his injury.

"Holy hell, Donnan. What happened?"

Torrian said, "He's gone. I see two men. We need to follow…" He turned toward his horse, just now noticing Donnan's wound. "Hellfire."

He couldn't speak. The words would not come. Wika reached his side and started to whine, pawing at his leg.

Torrian put his arm around his shoulder and said, "Lie down under the tree. I'll check your injury. I've spent enough time around my stepmother to know how to end the bleeding."

Logan said, "I'm going for help. We'll never get him to stay on a horse. I'm going back for Brenna. If I ride at full speed, I can have her back here in less than an hour. We aren't that far out."

One of the guards asked, "Are you sure we're not closer to Edinburgh? I'll head there and find a healer."

"Nay!" Donnan shouted. Every face turned to him. "Bethia. Do not bring Brenna. I want Bethia. Only Bethia."

"My sister treats animals, not people," Torrian said. "He needs to bring my mother."

Donnan shook his head. "Bethia is the only one I'll allow to touch me. Or I'll accept this as my time to go. Just tell Bethia I'm sorry I didn't get him."

Logan said, "I'm leaving. I'll bring Bethia back." He gave curt instructions to two of the guards who'd accompanied them, telling them to follow the marauders as far as they could. He flicked the reins of his horse, pointed to another guard to follow him, and left.

"Wait," Torrian yelled. "Take the dogs back with you. Wika, Morda, go!" Wika whined a bit, but she followed Logan after Donnan echoed the suggestion.

Torrian got him settled then lifted his tunic to see the wound clearly. "Donnan, you need stitching. I hope Bethia can do it."

"If she can sew an animal, she can sew me." He closed his eyes because Torrian's image had gone blurry, something he knew was bad.

Torrian said, "This is going to hurt, but Brenna always says to push on a wound. It helps stanch the bleeding."

"Do what you must." He could feel his strength waning. "The dogs?" He couldn't remember where they'd gone.

"Wika and Morda went with Logan. They're fine."

Donnan glanced off to the side, looking for Shewolf, hoping her wound wasn't bad enough to kill her, but he didn't see her anywhere. "Torrian. I can feel this is not good. I've lost a lot of blood, have I not?"

"Aye, you're bleeding heavily, but 'tis slowing. Close your eyes if you must. I'll awaken you when Bethia arrives. Conserve your strength."

Donnan closed his eyes for a moment, but then jerked his head back up. "Torrian, 'twas him."

"The one who stabbed you? You know him?"

"Aye, 'twas the same one who hurt Wynda. Scar on his face. And…" His eyes closed again. He just couldn't stay awake.

"Donnan. What?"

He opened his eyes and said, "I struck him in the shoulder with my sword. He's wounded. On horseback."

"You did? Well done. 'Twill slow him down. Now close your eyes and wait for my sister."

He didn't argue.

CHAPTER NINE

ᔥ

BETHIA WAS INSIDE THE STABLES checking on Bretta and her new pups when she heard the shouting. Out of habit, she grabbed her satchel and ran toward the gates. Her uncle and another guard were headed toward them in a full gallop, two dogs trailing them. The gates had been opened in preparation.

"Get Bethia," was all she heard. She increased her pace.

"What is it?"

Cailean and Sorcha, who'd been in the courtyard, were directly behind her. "Papa?" Sorcha yelled.

He stopped his horse in front of them and managed to get out, "Donnan's hurt. He's been stabbed and he wants you."

Bethia's eyes widened, but she didn't move. "But…"

"I know your mother is the healer, but Donnan said he would only allow you to touch him. He needs stitches. Bring your poultices. Grab your cloak and extra clothes. We won't be back for a while and the nights are cold. Sorcha, I'm taking Cailean with me. If you wish to come, you may. You're probably safest near that wild beast of a husband of yours, and I could use an archer. We're not certain, but I think that bastard Bearchun's out there and he has a decent archer shooting. MacAdam, find me three or four more guards. He went to Edinburgh, I believe, and I aim to follow him once this is finished. Donnan is closer to Edinburgh than he is to the keep, so I'll wait to make the call on who returns to Ramsay land until you've treated him, Bethia."

"I'll find my brother and his friends," Cailean said. "Sorcha? You're coming, wife. I need you with me. Get what you need from the keep." He started to leave before turning back and shouting,

"Please?"

Sorcha smirked, and she and Bethia headed off toward the keep.

Before they parted ways to go to their separate chambers, Bethia said, "Sorcha, leggings. I need a pair of leggings for under my gown, please." Her Aunt Gwyneth's creations were the best protection from the cold.

Sorcha nodded and slipped away.

Once in her chamber, Bethia moved without thinking, grabbing the bag she kept packed for emergencies and a warm cloak. As soon as she had what she needed, she left her chamber, ran through the great hall, and...

"Bethia?" her mother called to her. "What is it?"

"Uncle Logan wants me to tend to Donnan."

Her father, who stood behind her mother said, "Repeat everything, please."

"Uncle Logan said Donnan was stabbed by a man they think is Bearchun. Donnan's asking for me to stitch him. Uncle said we might be headed to Edinburgh afterward to catch Bearchun. Sorcha and Cailean are riding with us."

"Do you want me to go with you?" her mother asked.

Quade said, "Nay. I'll not have you both out there if Bearchun's still loose. Bethia, you may go, but you will return once you've done your stitching. I don't like the idea of you going to Edinburgh without a sound reason. I'll speak to your uncle while you get your things." He glanced at her mother. "I'll make sure he's taking enough guards for her."

Her mother said, "Quade, please do not go." The worry on her mother's face broke her heart. "Logan and Torrian can handle it."

Her sire wrapped his arms around her mother and said, "I'm not going anywhere. My knee prevents it, and I have faith in my brother and our son. But I must speak to Logan, remind him of what's at stake. You know how his temper controls him at times." He kissed her quickly, grabbed his wooden cane, and headed out the door.

"Bethia, do you think you can stitch a person?" her mama asked. "You've done small ones before..."

"Aye, I'll do whatever I have to. I just hope 'tis only skin. If 'tis too deep, I'll be lost."

"Nay, you'll not. Just stitch all the large vessels that are leak-

ing first, then sew the wound in layers if it's large. Otherwise, the
stitches will not hold. I'll get my poultice and some finer nee-
dles for you. The seepage needs to be stopped. You know the rest
of what Grandmama and Grandpapa taught me. Wash and plenty
of poultice." Her mother kissed her forehead, then took Bethia's
cloak from her hand and wrapped it around her shoulders. "Go,
time is of the essence if he's bleeding."

Bethia nodded, grabbed her satchel headed to the door just as
Sorcha raced down the staircase. "I brought the leggings for you,
Bethia."

"The extra heavy ones?" her mother asked.

"Aye. I have two for each of us."

Her mother said to Bethia, "Put one pair on before you leave.
No one will see you."

Bethia did as she suggested. Her mother kissed both of them
and said, "Go and Godspeed. If you need help, Bethia, Torrian has
assisted me many times."

As Bethia stumbled out the door, she realized she was finally taking part in one of her clan's quests. In the past, she'd never wished
to get involved, afraid of what might happen.

But this was different. Donnan wanted her, and she couldn't
let him down. As she walked across the courtyard with Sorcha, it
occurred to her that Donnan might not make it—a thought that
made her quite ill. True, there could be nothing between them
because Donnan had pledged never to marry again, but she wasn't
sure she could give her heart to anyone other than that kind, intelligent bear of a man…

Sorcha interrupted her thoughts. "Are you all right with this,
cousin?"

Bethia lifted her gaze to Sorcha's and nodded. "I have to be."

"You'll do a great job on Donnan. I think he's kind of handsome, but then I do like rugged-looking men, not lads. Think of
Cailean. Naught soft about him at all." She giggled and glanced
over at Bethia. "Sorry, Bethia. I know how difficult this is for you.
It was awful when Cailean took ill at the Grants. I'll help you if
I'm able. And when Donnan's hale and hearty, I'll make sure he
realizes he'd be a fool to let you go."

Oh, her cousin was dear to her…

Cailean stood near the stables with two horses. "Hurry, Sorcha.

Your sire is barking at me like a daft man looking to hang someone from the portcullis."

As if on cue, her father's voice rang out across the yard. "Never mind, MacAdam. Get my daughter mounted. Alan can assist Bethia."

Before she had time to consider all that had transpired, they mounted up and rode out of the gates.

Bethia's stomach twisted in a knot, afraid of what she would find. She said a quick prayer to keep Donnan alive until she got there.

☾

Donnan awakened to yelling, his mind hazy as he tried to recollect where he was at the moment. The pain in his side reminded him, his hand going to up to guard his injury without thinking.

Torrian knelt beside him. "Over here, Bethia," he shouted. The thunder of hooves told him there was a new group of horses approaching. The only other voice he recognized was Logan's, giving his instructions to the guards in the area.

He stared at the stars and their soft light in the sky. His thinking wasn't as clear as usual, but he guessed that was to be expected. Then *she* appeared in his vision, looking like an angel, her bright eyes and smile filling him with hope. She sat on a plaid her brother had placed next to Donnan's side, tucking her legs underneath her, her gown surrounding her.

"Donnan? Tell me what you feel." She reached for his right hand, squeezing it as a matter of comfort, he guessed. He tried to squeeze back. His left hand still guarded his wound.

She had a clean cloth on her lap and a satchel next to her.

"Dagger wound. About the length of my hand." He peeled his hand away so she could look at it. "Too much blood."

He watched her face, noticing she showed no disgust or revulsion at the sight of his bleeding, gore-stained wound, something that had almost turned his own belly. She used a linen strip to soak up the blood around the wound. "Your bleeding is not too heavy. My guess is Torrian did a good job pushing on it, aye? Mama always taught us to do so right away."

He nodded as she rambled. Hellfire, but when had he progressed to the point of falling in love with the lass? He hadn't thought it possible for him to believe in love again, but this woman was beginning to soften his edges. She was threatening to break down all his remaining walls. His heart ached nearly as much as his injury just from looking at her, just from thinking that she wasn't his, just from wanting her more than anything in the Highlands. He'd thought himself in love with Glenna, at least at first, but his feelings for her hadn't been anything like the need he fought for Bethia. He was drawn to her like a thousand bees to their queen. Her aura was so powerful, even his dogs and the wild wolf recognized it.

He needed Bethia in his life. To converse with, to touch, to love, and—could he be so lucky?—to be loved in return. That love had been missing in his life.

Glenna had never loved him. She'd only loved him for the wealth he'd been born into. Only loved him because he was…

"Donnan, I must sew your wound. I can give you something to ease the pain." She fussed with the tools she'd laid out next to her.

He shook his head. "Just sew. I can handle it." He knew how gentle her touch would be, and had so much faith in this slight woman that he'd trust her to do anything to him.

Logan came into his vision. "Bethia, can you repair it?"

She smiled at Donnan before answering her uncle. "I believe so."

Logan continued to stare at Bethia, and Donnan noticed that Torrian and a couple of other people stood directly behind her, looking on. "Uncle Logan, could someone please fetch me some fresh water?" Bethia asked. "Is there a burn nearby?"

"I'll get it, Logan," one of the guards responded.

She then settled her hands in her lap and turned to face the onlookers. "I believe I can repair Donnan's injury, but it would be most helpful if I didn't have an audience standing over my shoulder. I am unaccustomed to sewing people, so this will be a bit unnerving to me. I ask that you stand back and not hover."

"Agreed," Torrian said with a nod, "we'll move back, but I'd like someone to stay close by in case you need an extra hand. You choose your assistant."

"Torrian, you may stay, but off to the opposite side, not over my shoulder, if you please."

"Go ahead, lass. I trust you." Donnan gulped, praying she'd be quick about it.

"Donnan, I can give you some herbs to lessen the pain," she reminded him.

He shook his head adamantly. "Nay. I need my senses."

"All right. If you change your mind, just say so."

"I'd take a quick sip of aught you have, Torrian, before she begins."

Logan moved to his horse. "I grabbed a skin of ale. Drink up." He handed it over to Donnan, who took a large swig before returning it.

"That'll do me fine." He nodded to Bethia, indicating he was ready for her to begin.

CHAPTER TEN

B ETHIA WIPED THE SWEAT FROM her brow as she tore the tunic Donnan wore, revealing his chest and his belly. She had to have a view of all she was to work on, though she hadn't expected it to affect her in the manner it did.

He had a spattering of coarse, dark hairs across his chest and down the center toward the top of his plaid. The biggest difference between Donnan and all the animals she worked on? Donnan was sheer muscle, and glancing at his flesh heated her insides, warming her in a way she'd never experienced before.

She forced herself to focus. "I'll be as quick as I can, but I must sew this small vessel inside you before I work on your skin. 'Tis paramount that I stop that from bleeding. I believe 'tis the major source of all the blood you have lost."

She threaded her needle and said to Torrian, "Hold the torch closer so I can see better, please."

Torrian did as she asked, but as soon as she reached into the gore, he turned his head away.

"Torrian, will you be able to hold it?"

"Aye, I just cannot watch."

She understood that what she did was not for everyone. As a younger lass, her own stomach had turned a couple of times when she'd assisted her mother with one injury or another. It was a matter of determination and steadfastness. She would do this for this man she had grown so fond of in such a short time.

The thought surprised her, but it shouldn't have. Seeing him in such a condition had brought her feelings to the forefront. How she wished things could be different between them.

She placed another stitch, pulling it through, the muscle in his belly clenching from the pain, she was certain. Her mother oft told her pain on the inside was much stronger than pain on the outside. "I'm almost finished with the vessel, then you can have another swig of ale before I start joining the edges of the skin. He used a sharp blade on you, so the edges are not too jagged. I think 'twill go smoothly." She glanced up and caught his gaze, surprised at what she saw there.

Donnan cared for her, too.

He watched her with the same quiet strength she'd seen in her sire's gaze when he watched her mother from afar. Her father trusted her mother completely, and his eyes were always full of admiration, trust, and faith when he looked at her.

She could see those same emotions in Donnan's gaze. The ends of her lips curved just enough to let him know she was confident in what she did, that she could sew him and, hopefully, save his life.

With that one look, she hoped she could show him how much she wanted him, no, needed him to survive.

Then she looked down and got to work. Her hands were steadied by her determination to help him, and the stitch held true. "There. That vessel is finished. I'll move on to closing the wound. May I have the water, please?"

Cailean handed her the vessel filled from the burn while Logan gave Donnan another swig of ale. She thanked Cailean and tipped the contents over the wound. "I need to get any debris out before I start to sew. Forgive me, Donnan." He flinched, but only once, so she took a deep breath and finished what she needed to do. She handed the jug back to Cailean and asked, "More, please? I'll need more when I finish."

She caught Donnan's gaze and asked, "Ready? This will take longer. If you need me to stop at all, just say so."

"Get on with it, Bethia. I trust you completely."

How she wished she could kiss him before she continued. She so admired his quiet strength. Positioning her hand so the edges of the wound would be easy to gather, she pierced his flesh with the needle. He started from the pain, his hand was not far from her leg. "Donnan, grab my knee if you must. You'll not hurt me the way I'm hurting you. I'd give you my hand, but they're both busy." She waited for her uncle or her brother to argue with her, but neither did. Uncle Logan had been through enough to know exactly how much Donnan was suffering.

He squeezed her knee, and that connection motivated her to finish her task with a speed and agility that surprised her. She placed two layers of stitches in the first part of the wound, where the dagger had dug in deeper, but only one layer was necessary for the second section.

She sweated profusely, and at one point Donnan grabbed a stretch of his plaid and mopped her forehead to keep it from dripping into her eyes. His concern for her made her heart swell. Close to an hour later, she placed her last stitch and whispered, "Finished, Donnan. All I must do is cover it with poultice and wrap a stretch of linen around it. We must keep it clean and hold it tight so the stitches don't pop out."

"Whatever you say," he said. "My thanks to you, Bethia."

She smiled at him. "You're welcome. Let's hope I did a good job." When she finished bandaging him up, she reached up to Torrian and her brother helped her stand. She almost toppled over as soon as she was completely on her feet. "My goodness. My knees seemed to have locked up on me. Pardon, but I'd like a moment alone at the stream."

She didn't wait for permission but moved straight toward the burn, ignoring the pain in her one knee from Donnan's tight grip. Had she done enough? Tears slid down her cheek, even though she tried to stop them. She knelt in front of the stream, placing her hands in the cool fluid to wash them—as if the force of the water could wash away all her fears of what she'd done, or act in her mother's place and tell her she'd done a fine job.

Her mother was not here.

She cupped her hands into the cool water and splashed it on her face, hoping to wash away the evidence of her tears. When she scrubbed her face and opened her eyes, she sensed a presence. Turning her head, she noticed that she did indeed have company.

Donnan's wolf limped toward her.

"Do not move, Bethia," Torrian yelled. "One arrow will finish it."

Bethia held her hand up to her brother. "I know this animal. Do not shoot her."

"If she attacks or does aught aggressive, she's dead. Proceed with care."

Bethia nodded. Her gaze took in the arrow that still protruded from the wolf's flank. The animal stood still, her hind leg lifted in the air, she guessed from the pain of the injury. "Torrian, fetch my satchel and toss it next to me, please."

He did as she asked. While he took off, Bethia patted her lap and said, "Come. I will help you, my pretty Shewolf."

The beast panted, but didn't move. Her gaze was a bit clouded. Bethia wondered how much blood the wolf had lost. If she had to guess, she would say that Shewolf had tried to rid herself of the weapon, for the bulk of the arrow had broken off.

Torrian returned and tossed the bag toward her. She reached for the bag, never taking her eye off the wolf, and reaching inside for her numbing agent. She applied a small amount of the unguent onto her finger before returning the container to the bag and setting the bag down.

She beckoned the animal again. "Come, Shewolf."

The beast lowered her head and moved toward her. She didn't settle her head on her lap, but she did lay next to her—a position that brought the wound closer to Bethia.

She held her hand out and let the hurt creature smell her.

Torrian said, "Sister, you are not thinking. Even if she's tame with Donnan, she'll not let you treat her."

"Do not worry. We've met before."

The wolf licked the side of her hand.

"What the hell?" Torrian groaned out. "You *and* Lily?"

She slowly moved her hand toward the animal's wound and rubbed the salve around the outside of the injury, giving it a few minutes to do its work. The wolf slid closer and lay her head down, as if to let Bethia know the pain had finally eased. "I'm going to take that arrow out now, Shewolf, then I'll put more ointment on you." She set her hand near the wound to make sure the wolf would accept her help. Shewolf rolled her flank toward Bethia and her head in the opposite direction.

As if she understood.

Bethia didn't hesitate, but reached into the shallow wound to grab the edges of the arrowhead and extracted it. The beast jumped once, but she didn't growl or otherwise threaten her. She tossed the arrow off to the side, then hastily covered the wound with more of the unguent. Shewolf stood and limped over to the arrow, sniffed it, then glanced over her shoulder at her savior before she moved off into the bushes.

Torrian said, "Hell, I've never seen aught like it, lass."

"She visits Donnan often, came out when I checked on Wynda one day."

"I'll not question you again."

Her gaze followed the retreating animal. When she was out of sight, Bethia leaned forward to wash her hands in the stream again.

A hand pressed her shoulder, and she sat back on her heels to look up at her brother.

"You did a fine job on Donnan, I think. There's no more bleeding and he's alert." She reached for his hand and he helped her to stand again.

"My thanks. How did you know to check on me?"

"Because you are so like Brenna in all you do, and I recall how difficult it was for her when I was ill and she didn't know how to help me. Whenever she bathed my blisters, she would always cry afterward. I thought I heard tears before the wolf came to visit you."

She laughed. "She did? I was hoping to hide my tears."

"Aye. Sometimes I thought it hurt her more than it did me. I remember wondering what kind of person was strong enough to spend their lives causing others pain, even though they knew they were helping them."

"You did? Torrian, you were so young." She peered up at her strong brother, the laird. *His* strength inspired her every day. How she wished she dared to discuss Donnan with him, but he had more serious concerns than the affairs of his sister's heart.

"Aye, but I had quite a bit of time to think. 'Twas all I did."

Her voice dropped. "Not all you did. You were fighting for your life. You were an amazing young lad, from what Mama has told me."

"Mayhap," he grinned.

"My thanks for understanding."

"May I ask you a question?" He stood back with his arms crossed in front of him.

She nodded, unable to speak because she was sure the tears would start again once her brother spoke his mind. The nature of what he was about to ask would surely embarrass her, but she welcomed his guidance and was humbled that he cared about her small problems.

"Is there something between you and Donnan that I should know about?"

He never minced words. Tears misted in her eyes again, much as she hated them. "I could only wish. He says he'll never marry again. His losses were too painful for him to risk it. I respect his choice."

"Would you like me to speak with him? I will if it would please you."

"Nay. Please do not," she cried out. "I would not want our relationship to have such a start. I accept it for what it is, and I have learned from him."

Torrian stared at her, and she wished she could read his mind. She trusted her brother, but this was all so new for her, and she wasn't quite comfortable admitting she was close to losing her heart to Donnan.

"Torrian, time to move," Uncle Logan yelled their way.

The moment lost, they hurried back to the group clustered around a boulder. She was surprised to find Donnan sitting up. His wound was above the waist, but the pain and pressure had to be considerable.

"Your plan, Uncle Logan?" Torrian asked.

"Quite simple. The guards who followed Bearchun and his archer returned, and they confirmed they were headed toward Edinburgh. We'll follow them there. Donnan wounded Bearchun with his sword, so he'll be moving slower than usual, too. I've offered to send Donnan back to the keep, but he's refused. Bethia, what do you think?"

"Riding a horse will be difficult for you, Donnan," Bethia said, feeling her brow furrow. "You must do your best not to gallop or jar your wound."

"She's right," Logan said. "I watched my brother ride a distance a sennight after his stitches were placed and it was still a trial for him."

Donnan nodded. "I understand that. I'll safeguard the wound as much as possible, Now that you've closed it, it does not appear to be so large. I'd like to see this through, and if I still have my wits about me, the distance to Edinburgh is much shorter than the distance back to Ramsay land."

"It would be better for him to go to Edinburgh and rest a day or two before he travels the entire distance back to Ramsay land," Bethia said with a decisive nod.

Uncle Logan thought for a moment, then said, "I can arrange that. I'll see him settled at an inn before I seek out Bearchun."

"We could use you since you've seen the bastard most recently," Torrian said, nodding at Donnan. "Bethia? Pack your satchel. I'm sending you back to the keep with a guarded escort."

Bethia barked out a very loud, "Nay."

All faces turned toward her, so she did her best to speak with confidence, her eyes locked with the gaze of her shrewd uncle. "If Donnan goes, I go. It's imperative that he not re-open his wound." She didn't glance at Donnan, but she did catch the surprise in her uncle's and Sorcha's eyes. True, she tended not to travel outside of Ramsay land, and if she did, it was usually only to Grant or Cameron land. In truth, she'd never considered the possibility of leaving.

Her uncle snorted and said, "You are returning home. I promised your sire I'd send you back as soon as you were finished with Donnan."

"Well, you can inform my sire of the truth upon our return. I'm not finished with Donnan."

Every set of eyes widened and there were a few slack jaws in the group, but she was not deterred.

"He'll not tear my stitches," she announced to all, and no one argued.

CHAPTER ELEVEN

ↄ

THEY MADE IT TO EDINBURGH in a couple of hours. Donnan was glad of it, because he had a sudden need to sleep, and
he doubted he would have been able to sit his horse for much
longer. He'd vowed not to ruin Bethia's careful stitchery. He'd
been mighty proud of her for taking a stand against her uncle.
Many a guard lacked the gumption and strength of character she'd
demonstrated.

Logan stopped and spoke to the group. "Here's my suggestion.
See if you agree with me, Torrian. I'd like to take the guards and
move through the burgh, see what we can discover. It's still the
middle of the night, so I'd suggest Donnan and the women get
some sleep in the inn. I'll leave you and Cailean as their protection.
We'll return in several hours, then regroup. We need to find him
before his trail goes cold, though I suspect he's found a place to
hide and get himself some stitches, so we may not find him until
the morrow."

"I can go along," Torrian said.

"Nay. We have two prime targets for him—Bethia and Sorcha.
In fact we have over a dozen guards, while he traveled with only
one. I'll leave some with you and the others go with me. We'll
return before high noon to decide our next move. 'Tis my guess
he's here to hire men, but now he's slowed with an injury. I'll
check with the known healers."

Torrian nodded. "Find us a quality inn, Uncle, one that is often
frequented by women. You know the area best."

Donnan didn't argue either. If he didn't get some rest, he'd be
falling off his horse. He had been familiar with Edinburgh many

years ago, and prayed he would not see anyone who would recognize him.

Logan led them to an inn in the middle of the city. The two
groups split up, and Cailean lifted Donnan off his horse, not waiting for his approval. He nodded his thanks, grabbing ahold of the
big warrior's shoulder to regain his balance. As soon as Donnan
was steady on his feet, Cailean moved on to lift Sorcha down while
Torrian assisted Bethia. After Torrian gave the guards instructions,
he approached the door and spoke to the man keeping watch. A
few moments later, he gestured for the others to follow him inside.

Though Donnan managed to walk through the door by himself,
he immediately sunk into a chair by the door. He needed food or
water, something. As if she'd read his mind, Bethia located an ewer
of water on a side table and poured him a goblet, bringing it to
him. "Mama says you must fight fever with water," she said sweetly.

The inn was quite large, and after a short discussion with the
innkeeper, Torrian followed the portly man down a long passageway, indicating for them to follow him. Cailean moved the two
lasses in front of him before falling into line behind them. Donnan
lifted himself, with some difficulty, and trailed after the group. The
passage had several heavy sconces that lit their path, an indication
of an establishment of a certain quality. The innkeeper held the
door open and stood back, waving his hand with a flourish. "Our
best chambers, my lord. We save this area for those who do not
wish to mix with the others in the inn. 'Tis more private."

Torrian checked the condition of the chambers before moving
them inside. He said something else to the innkeeper, then turned
to Cailean, "Get everyone settled," he said, "and you can guard the
door until I return. I'm going to check outside again."

Sorcha wandered through the rooms and then whistled. "There
are three separate chambers with beds," she announced.

Cailean pointed to the bed in the small chamber to the left and
said, "Donnan, there's only one bed in there. 'Tis yours."

He couldn't get there fast enough. He mumbled a quick thanks,
closed the door behind him and managed to pull off his plaid
before he fell into the bed and closed his eyes, falling fast asleep,
only to dream about a beautiful brown-eyed lass.

C

When Donnan awakened, the sun was almost at its peak. He'd slept half the day away, something he never did. He checked his wound, pleased to see that the stitches were intact and he didn't appear to be bleeding any more. There was only dried blood on the linen strips.

He remembered Bethia's insistence on keeping Wynda's wound clean, so he decided he should do the same. He stepped into the main gathering area, furnished with a table and four chairs and a washing table off to the side, and was surprised to find it empty. He knew the area well enough, so he decided to find the bathing house down the street. He'd get an ale, mayhap a meat pie from a street vendor, then bathe.

He ran into Torrian just outside the inn. The laird had an ale in his hand, which he quickly handed off to Donnan.

"My thanks. I needed something." After several swallows, he returned the skin to Torrian, wiping his mouth.

"Where are you headed? We can get food at the inn. 'Tis where the others are awaiting my uncle."

"Bethia advised me on the importance of keeping a wound clean. I'm off to the bathing house."

"Donnan, forgive me for being nosy, but she is my sister. Do you have any intentions toward her?"

Donnan didn't know what to say. He stared down the street, thinking carefully before he answered. "I've never met anyone like your sister, and that includes my wife. I admit I am interested, but I don't think 'twould be fair to your sister, given my past."

"I understand your concern, but don't you think she's mature enough to make that decision on her own? Why not court her and see if the two of you suit? I can see my sister is interested in you."

Donnan ran his hand down his beard. "Do you think she would consider me?"

Torrian chuckled. "I think so, but may I offer a piece of advice?"

He dropped his hand to his side, surprised Torrian had agreed. He'd little expected the laird would want him—Daft Donnan—as his sister's suitor. "Of course."

"You might want to trim your hair and your beard. Lassies aren't so fond of all that extra hair." He winked at Donnan and patted his shoulder as he stepped past him and made his way into the inn.

Donnan had been thinking the same thing.

☪

In the middle of the afternoon, Sorcha and Bethia decided to seek out more refreshments. Cailean was hungry, as usual. It had been a long, boring day, and Donnan still had not returned to the inn.

"How much longer do you think we'll be here?" Bethia asked.

"My guess is Papa will be back before dark, and we'll either go home or spend one more night here. I doubt he's been able to find Bearchun. The lout has been elusive for quite some time. I doubt he'd be this easy to catch."

"I hope Donnan's all right. 'Tis too soon for the fever to start, but he has not eaten much. He's been gone far too long."

"You do like him, aye? I can see it in you whenever he's near."

Bethia didn't know how to answer. She should be truthful, but it would be quite embarrassing when Sorcha learned that Donnan did not return her interest. She sighed and plowed ahead with the truth, something her mother had taught her was always best. "Aye, 'tis true that I'm interested in him, but he says he'll never marry again." She wasn't sure how much Sorcha knew of his past, so she told her all she knew.

"Oh, how awful. The poor man. I feel so horrible for him," Sorcha said.

"Now you understand why he'll never remarry."

"But you would never leave him. You're as loyal and faithful as anyone I know."

Bethia smiled. "Thank you, though I doubt it matters much to him."

They'd almost made it to the dining hall when Sorcha giggled and whispered in her ear. "I would so love to see what he looks like underneath all that hair."

Bethia giggled just as the door behind them opened. She turned her head to see who'd stepped inside—and immediately froze.

Sorcha noted her reaction and spun around to the door. "Oh my heavens."

Bethia couldn't speak.

Donnan stood in front of them, unmoving, as they both stared at him. "Is something wrong?"

They both shook their heads, Sorcha reacting faster than she did. Then Bethia broke out into a wide smile. "Donnan, you look quite handsome." She blushed, but she couldn't help but express her pleasure. It was as if Sorcha's words had conjured the sight before them. Donnan had shaved off his beard and cut his hair, and she'd never seen anyone as handsome. If he walked into the Ramsay great hall looking like he did right now, he'd have several lasses swooning. His face was so smooth, she wished to reach up and rub the back of her hand across it. After staring a wee bit too much, she managed to get control of her emotions. The gray of his eyes stood out even more now that they weren't hidden behind his hair and the bushiness of his beard. In fact, they seemed to be dancing in merriment at the moment. He was probably amused by her comment.

Sorcha whispered, "I knew he'd look better, but I never would have guessed…"

"I beg your pardon?" Donnan asked.

"Naught," Sorcha said. "Naught. Aye, you look fine without the beard. And your hair was trimmed nicely." She continued to stare wide-eyed at him.

Bethia wasn't surprised. She knew *she* couldn't stop staring. "We're headed to the kitchens for some meat pies. Would you care to join us?"

"Aye. I am a bit hungry." He smiled.

Bethia motioned for Sorcha to move on ahead of them and beckoned to Donnan. His lips were fuller than she'd realized, and his teeth were so white.

Focus, Bethia, she chastened herself.

"How is your wound?"

"I removed the bandage and washed it. I didn't see anything green yet. The stitches are still in place. Must I look for aught else besides green?"

"Well, sometimes the seepage can turn a thick white before the fever sets in. When we return upstairs, I'll put more salve on it and redress it."

"Aye, my thanks."

Now that he'd shaved, she noticed something else about him, one of the signs her mother had taught her to look for in her patients. He was quite pale, not a good sign, and she could see a fine tremor in his hand. "Does it hurt much?"

"Just a wee bit. 'Tis tolerable. I have an appetite, which is an improvement." One of the serving girls brought out a tray of meat pies, cheese, and a loaf of bread. Bethia had been so wrapped up in her conversation with Donnan that she hadn't heard Sorcha make the request.

"Perfect," Sorcha said. "The bread smells wonderful. Cailean is always hungry. I can carry it. Many thanks."

They moved back to their chambers and the three stepped inside the main one.

"Holy shite," Cailean yelled.

"What is it?" Sorcha asked. "Do not scare me, or I'll drop the tray."

He pointed to Donnan. "Is that really you, Donnan? You look so different."

"Where's my brother?" Bethia asked.

"He'll be right back. He went off in search of Logan. Took some guards with him."

"Donnan, I know you're hungry, but I should dress that wound first." Bethia turned to her satchel. "I'll get my things. If you wish to lie down, I'll be quick about it so you can eat."

Donnan nodded and returned to the room he'd occupied the night before. Bethia followed him in, closing the door behind her, though she could still hear Cailean talking.

"Shouldn't we...should we open the door?" he asked Sorcha. "They're not married. Torrian would supervise."

"Nay," she heard her cousin say. "Leave them be. If my sire or Torrian comes in, I'll open the door quickly."

She'd thank her cousin for that later.

Apparently, Donnan had also overheard them. "I'm not in any position to hurt you, lass. You're not worried, are you?"

She blushed and shook her head, fussing over her supplies. "I don't see much blood. Did you wash much away?"

"Nay. 'Twas mostly dried blood. You did a fine job. I'm grateful to you for coming to me last eve. I trust you, Bethia." He sat on the side of the bed facing her, sitting up as straight as possible, probably because it eased the pain a bit.

She moved a stool over to him, settling her tools within her reach. Once she found what she needed, she leaned back and gazed down at him.

She promptly dropped her tool.

Hell. Unlike Sorcha, she did not typically use the lads' filthy talk, but that was the only word that came to mind. Donnan was the handsomest man she'd ever set her gaze upon. Now that his beard was gone, his smooth skin called to her in a way she knew not how to control.

"Lass?"

His gaze caught hers and she swallowed, trying her best to come up with any intelligible remark. "May I…would you mind…"

The corners of his lips curved upward in a slight smile. "I'm yours, Bethia Ramsay." The look he gave her and the husky tone he used shot straight to her core—deep and low enough to make her nearly pant with need. "Do as you wish with me."

A thousand visions of her lips on him in various places crossed her mind, startling her own sense of decency enough to make her blush.

"Bethia?"

She still hadn't moved. The only place she wished to move was closer. His hand reached up and stroked her cheek.

In a voice that caressed her insides the same way his hand caressed her cheek, he said, "You'll have to come to me, or I'll burst your stitches."

She almost fell on him, but he righted her at the last moment as her lips found their way to his, her tongue mating with his in a most inappropriate, delicious way. He suckled her tongue until she moaned, causing her to pull away, but not far.

She still hadn't done what she needed to do. Holding herself as close as she could without pressing her body to his, she reached up to touch his smooth cheek.

"You are glad I shaved?" His teeth nipped at her lower lip, but he held back, allowing her to do as she wished.

"Aye," she whispered.

"I'll shave every day if you'll look at me like that again."

"Donnan, I need to…"

"Go ahead. Whatever you like…"

She kissed his cheek, running her tongue roughly across his jaw-line and up to his ear, teasing him a bit there before she sat back in shock at what she'd just done. Her hand came up to her mouth and she dropped her gaze to the floor, suddenly mortified.

"Och, nay, you'll not disappear on me, woman." He grasped her shoulder and tugged her lips to his, devouring her mouth, roughly ravaging her with his tongue, his hand kneading the skin on the back of her neck until she wished to scream from pleasure. Her face fell to his neck as she did her best to slow her breathing.

However, when she took the time to notice, she discovered he was panting as badly as she was.

The realization empowered her. Donnan wanted her as much as she wanted him. His hand trailed a path around her cheeks until his thumb found her bottom lip. Her tongue slid out to taste him, and she lifted her gaze to his to see how he would react.

A growl came from deep within him, but then he abruptly turned his head away from her. "Bethia, there's naught I would rather do right now than pleasure you on this bed until you scream my name, and trust me that if the time ever comes for us, you will scream my name *ten* times before I finish, but 'tis not right." He turned back toward her and reached for her hand. "We have to stop before I cannot. I will not disrespect you that way."

The door flew open and Uncle Logan barged in the chamber with his hands on his hips, Torrian directly behind him. He took one look at Bethia and leapt at Donnan, planting his fist at his jaw. He then picked him up and tossed him across the chamber. Donnan hit the wall and crumpled to the floor, grabbing his midsection.

Her uncle went after him again.

CHAPTER TWELVE

ᘐ

DONNAN MANAGED TO PUSH HIMSELF up off the floor though he knew he'd torn stitches. He'd felt them give way, could feel the blood seeping through the bandage.

He hated himself for what he'd done to an innocent, but he was also furious. Bethia was of an age to make up her own mind. Logan came at him again, and this time he strong-armed the smaller man, pushing him back with all his might, but it didn't stop the man's tirade. "You bastard. That's my niece, my gentle niece you are playing with. How dare you touch her." A fist came at Donnan again, and he managed to duck enough to drive a blow of his own into Logan's belly, but he didn't have enough strength to do much damage.

But the screams of a sweet lass stopped them both. "Stop it, stop it, Uncle Logan. He cannot fight. What the hell is your problem?"

"You swore at me?" Logan swung around to stare at Bethia, his eyes round with wonder. "You cursed! My dear niece cursed at me. What the hell have you done to her?"

And Donnan was even angrier. "Do not take that tone with her, Ramsay. I care not if she's your niece. She deserves your respect."

Logan spun back around to face him again. "You dare speak to me so? You had your hands all over her. She's an innocent."

"She has desires, just as any other lass of twenty summers would. My hands never touched below her neck."

Bethia shouted, "Stop it, both of you! Uncle Logan, you'll kill him. Look how he's already bleeding. He's ripping all my stitches."

Logan lunged for him. "I'll rip more stitches, you bastard. Nay, she does not have desires. 'Tis Bethia, my sweet Bethia. Do not teach her your filthy ways."

Filthy? The man was addled!

Torrian came between them, reaching for Logan and pulling him off Donnan. Panting with exertion from holding his wild uncle, he said, "Cailean, stand in front of Donnan. *Now.*"

Logan fought hard against Torrian's powerful arms. "MacAdam, stay the hell out of this, or you'll pay later."

Cailean's eyebrows shot up, and he took a step toward Donnan, apparently listening to his laird. But his gaze also gauged his distance from his father-in-law.

"MacAdam, your laird gave you an order. Don't move." Cailean stood fast, holding his hands behind his back.

"Uncle Logan, what the hell *is* your problem?" Torrian asked. "They're both fully clothed. I was directly behind you and saw naught untoward or askew. What the hell could have happened? And my sister is no longer a bairn, may I remind you."

Logan continued his tirade. "I could see it in both their eyes. His hands were all over her, and she was falling for whatever bull he was handing her. He'll not violate her. You're their laird, Torrian. Do something. She's your sister."

Donnan stepped away from Cailean, his hand guarding his injury, and faced Torrian. "I'd like to ask for your sister's hand in marriage." Hellfire, he'd fallen for the lass, and fallen hard. Though the thought of marriage still scared him, he meant every word.

He didn't miss the wide-eyed look on Bethia's face or how her jaw dropped open. Would she agree? The pain in his side suddenly seemed unimportant, his attention was fully focused on Bethia and whether or not she would accept his backhanded proposal.

Logan said, "Damn right, you'll marry her. How dare you touch her right in front of me. We'll find a priest now." Yanking himself free from Torrian's hold, he started pacing. "I won't touch him again, but don't confine me. I'm still your uncle and a hell of a lot older and smarter than you."

Torrian quirked his brow at his uncle and shouted, "Fine. Pace all you please, but do you truly think you're smarter? You sure aren't demonstrating it at the moment."

Logan put his face up to his nephew's. "Are you going to let him touch your sister like that?"

Without moving his face, Torrian asked, "Bethia, did Donnan

hurt you or do aught inappropriate?"

"Nay. We only kissed, and I'll kiss whomever I want, Uncle Logan. I started it," Bethia retorted.

Logan's hands went to his head, as if he could not believe what his ears had told him. "What have you done to her? You truly are daft, Donnan. You've corrupted my sweetest niece. You'll marry her, and then I'll keep the two of you in separate places. You can go back to living in the wild, and she'll stay sweet and innocent. Do you hear me?"

Another wave of fury washed over Donnan, but before he could say aught, a loud scream interrupted them. It didn't stop until they all turned to look at her.

Bethia stood with her face raised toward the rafters, her mouth open wide as she bellowed, her eyes lit with fury. Donnan had never seen anything more beautiful.

She ended her scream and dropped her voice to a whisper. "How *dare* you. How dare you all decide what's right for me without even asking me what I want. Uncle Logan, I'll not marry anyone just because you say so. And mayhap you should try talking to *me* once in a while. If you did, you'd discover that I'm tired of being the innocent in the family. All my younger cousins are getting married, and until a few days ago, I'd never been kissed. Well, guess what? Now I have. And I'll tell you something else. I liked it."

Donnan had never seen so many shocked expressions in his life. He stood in the back of the chamber with a small grin on his face, hoping Bethia would continue. She was magnificent in her wrath. A small burst told him what his heart already knew. He loved this strong woman in front of him. He had no idea what she was about to say, but he knew, without a doubt, that she would speak her mind. She was as steadfast as any person could be, something he treasured about her. Had he ever known another like her?

"And Donnan, how dare you ask him…" Her finger pointed to her brother. "Before you ask me? I make my own decisions from now on. No one will tell me what to do. I'm a grown woman, and I know what I want. At the present, I wish to get away from all of you…" She turned and fled the sleeping chamber, tears falling down her face. A door opened and slammed, her sobs could be heard all the way down the passageway.

They all stared through the open doorway of the little sleeping chamber. Logan said, "Don't just stand there, Cailean. Go after her. If I do, I'll keep yelling. Sorcha, go talk with her and bring her back. Protect them both, Cailean. Bearchun is still out there. Make sure five guards follow her." He reached up and tugged on his hair. "Nieces, daughters…how many more do I have?" Cailean and Sorcha hurried out the door.

Donnan closed his eyes.

He was a horse's arse. He'd trampled her will just as the others had done.

(

Bethia ran and ran until she had nowhere else to go. She found a rock and sat on it in a huff, but it was so cold on her bottom, even through her leggings, that she jumped back up and cursed. "Hellfire!"

Cursing felt quite good, really. Now she understood why Sorcha could not stop herself.

She paced the small area opposite the inn. Horses were everywhere, but she ignored them, even though a few soft whinnies called to her.

Just as they always did.

She missed her animals. Dealing with them was far easier than dealing with people. Mayhap she should have stayed home.

But then she recalled how it felt to kiss Donnan, and how he'd allowed her to touch him as she pleased. How his hands had felt on her. He made her feel special. But some of the people she loved most of all had talked about her as if she weren't there. Uncle Logan, Torrian, and even Donnan…

She sobbed into her hands wondering how she could possibly speak to her brother or her uncle ever again. She'd been caught in a compromising position, something the elders in her family had always warned Maggie and Sorcha about, but never her. She'd kissed and cursed and sobbed and ran and…mayhap uncle Logan was right. What the hell *had* happened to her?

She faintly registered the sound of running feet, and before she could be alarmed, Sorcha appeared in front of her. "Bethia, I'm so sorry."

She wrapped her arms around Bethia's shoulders, and Bethia sobbed uncontrollably. When she was finally able to speak, she asked Sorcha, "What have I done?"

"Oh, Bethia. Just ignore my sire. He ranted at me the same way. You should have seen how cruel he was to Cailean."

"He was?" she said, her voice hitching.

"Aye. 'Tis just that you surprised everyone so. Cousin, you've never raised your voice before. Even I've never heard you speak in such a way." She took a step back and brushed a few strands of hair back from Bethia's wet cheeks.

"I know. They'll be so angry."

"Nay. You've just shown them something quite important. You've grown up, and my sire can't handle it. He may be angry, but trust me, 'twill not last forever. Know that I love you, and I am proud of you for standing up for yourself. Your mother would want you to be strong. You haven't the experience, but why not start now?"

Mayhap Sorcha had a point. Several Ramsay guards had fallen in around them, one of them Cailean. She dried her cheeks of tears when she saw her brother approaching. "Bethia, forgive me," he said as he stepped through the circle of guards. "Bearchun was seen in the area several hours ago, so I cannot allow you to stay out here."

He moved closer to her. "I'm so sorry. I trust you completely." He reached up to brush a tear that had escaped. "We'll talk more when we arrive back on Ramsay land. I want Papa to hear all you've said, too." He paused. "Well, mayhap not all," he added with a small smile.

She let out a deep sigh at the thought of explaining her actions to her father. "Must we? Can we not forget it all?"

"Nay. Donnan will ask Papa for your hand because 'tis his preference. I know you're upset, but Donnan is still bleeding and needs to be tended. Logan has reserved the hall in the inn for our dinner."

"I'll be right there." Her gaze dropped to the ground. How embarrassed she was over all that had transpired.

Torrian set his finger under her chin, lifting her gaze to his, and whispered, "I enjoyed seeing your temper. 'Tis time it came out. We all have the right to be angry when the situation calls for it. What you said was true, you are a woman fully grown. Uncle Logan will accept it, in time. But we must protect both you and Sorcha, so inside we go."

She nodded, gave Sorcha a quick hug, and then followed Torrian back inside.

Uncle Logan stood inside the entryway to the inn. "Bethia, forgive my loss of temper, but you've crossed a line. We'll be discussing marriage at a later time. Torrian will remain by your side while you repair Donnan's stitches."

She had no desire to speak to her uncle at the moment—and no ability to do so civilly—so she simply nodded to him and strode past him toward their chamber, feeling a fresh wave of fury.

Donnan sat on the edge of his bed, a cloth held against his wound. She lifted her chin and sat on the stool at his bedside. "My thanks for gathering my supplies," she said quietly. They'd been kicked about earlier, but he'd gathered them all into a neat pile.

Torrian came in and settled on another stool, her supervisor. She got up to retrieve a basin of water after washing her hands.

When she returned, she addressed Donnan. "Has the wound stopped bleeding?" She reached for the linen he held against it, but he stopped her with his hand.

"Nay, Bethia. You'll not continue until we settle this between us. I know this is a poor situation, but based on the circumstances, I ask you if you would do me the honor of becoming my wife." He reached for her hand, but she tugged it away.

She was angry with him as well. He and the others had made her feel as if she were a wee lass of ten summers, unable to understand what the older people did and completely ignorant of the ways of the world. Shouldn't he have proposed to her immediately after he ravaged her mouth instead of speaking to her brother as if she were not in their presence? "I appreciate that you are trying to right a perceived wrong, but I am not interested in accepting such a proposal."

Silence greeted her declaration. She shoved her stool back and crossed her arms. "Allow me to explain myself, Donnan, because you clearly know verra little about me."

The fury that had been foremost in her mind for the past hour took a step back, and a shocking calm took its place. Suddenly, she knew what needed to be said. "Donnan, our acquaintance has been short, so I can understand why you might make such a mistake, but Torrian, you and Uncle Logan disappoint me. You should both know better."

She noticed the form of her uncle moving to stand in the doorway of the main chamber, his gaze now on her.

"Mayhap I have lived a protected life, much of it by choice, but that doesn't give anyone else the right to make decisions for me. I was raised…" She paused for a moment to choke her tears back. "I was raised by two of the most wonderful parents a lass could have asked for. My parents raised me to believe that my mind is every bit as good as a man's. Aye, I have not traveled far from Ramsay land, but that does not make me a fool. I have a good mind. My father adores my mother and consults her whenever he needs to make a decision because he values her wisdom."

"Bethia," Uncle Logan said. "Please…"

"Nay, do not interrupt me, Uncle. Have enough respect for me to allow me to speak my mind. I remember my grandmama well, as should both of you." She pointed to Torrian and then her uncle. "Grandmama Arlene was a strong woman and did a fine job as the mistress of our clan. And my mother's mother made Uncle Alex promise to give the lasses in the Grant family a say on who they were to marry. I understand that many in the land would disagree with her forward thinking, but I did not expect any of *you* to treat me that way."

She paused to gather the strength to finish, her gaze traveling to meet Donnan's. Though she'd expected condemnation or anger, she saw only admiration. It helped her find the strength she needed to finish speaking her thoughts. "Donnan, I do not accept your proposal. It was made for all the wrong reasons, and I will not be forced into a marriage by anyone." She stood and moved over to her brother. "Brother, *I* have made the decision to refuse his proposal." Then she stomped over to her uncle. "Uncle Logan, I love you dearly, but you will *not* choose my husband for me. I kissed that man because I chose to. I do not regret that decision, but 'tis no reason for you to force a marriage. It was a kiss. I'll only marry a man who wants to marry me without any pushing. I've said all I care to say about this, and I don't want to hear it discussed until we are back in Ramsay keep, and then I…I will talk to my parents about it."

She spun on her heel and headed back to the stool.

"Wait, Bethia," Uncle Logan said, his voice surprisingly soft.

She paused, her chin lifted another notch.

He hugged her and said, "You are right. You have my apologies. I was in the wrong."

She returned his hug and said, "My thanks. Now I need to fix my stitchery."

"As soon as you're finished, meet us downstairs for dinner. Bearchun was in Edinburgh, but we lost his trail. As I said before, I believe he's found someone to keep him hidden while he consults a healer. If so, I'd prefer to keep him off guard. I want him to think we're spending the night in the inn, but we will move immediately after dark."

"Ride home in the dark?" Torrian asked.

Uncle Logan turned to leave but stopped at the door. "Someday you'll learn, nephew. No one knows this land better than I do. I've spent years traveling and roaming." He cast a glance at Bethia. "He can't surprise me."

CHAPTER THIRTEEN

ᛞ

DONNAN HAD EATEN ALMOST EVERY meal alone for the past two and a half years, and yet this felt like the quietest meal he'd ever endured. The tension was so thick it was nearly visible. Listening to Bethia lecture the three of them on her value as a woman had come as a rude awakening for him. He was ashamed of his behavior, especially since he *did* appreciate her.

He'd fallen in love with a very intelligent woman with a tender heart. When she'd finished repairing his stitches before dinner, he'd said, "My thanks for not taking your anger out on me with your needle."

She'd sighed and replied, "Donnan, if you even considered that possibility for a moment, then you truly know naught about me."

He'd lowered his voice and said, "But I'd like to know more."

Her shoulders had sagged a bit and she'd left him, gathering her things in preparation for their departure.

Nary a word had been spoken during the meal other than Logan and Torrian's continued conversation on Bearchun and his whereabouts.

All Donnan could think of was how he'd wronged Bethia and how desperate he was to fix it, although this was the wrong place. For the moment, he thought the best plan was to get Sorcha and Bethia safely back to Ramsay land, then he would approach Bethia before he spoke to her parents.

They left after the meal, the group still quiet. They had just reached to the outskirts of Edinburgh when the shouts of a man carried to them from down the road. "Stop, please!"

Donnan and the others tugged the reins of their horses.

"Halt, I say," the man cried out desperately.

Logan, who was in the front line of the group, said, "I'm Logan Ramsay. What is this about?" He glared at the intruder.

The man stopped next to Donnan and said incredulously, "I was correct. 'Tis truly you." He stared at Donnan.

Donnan's gut clenched in fear, true fear. Were all the secrets he'd worked so hard to protect about to be casually revealed by a stranger? He said a quick prayer that he'd be able to conceal his identity for a short time longer. He dared not speak for fear the tremor in his voice would give him away.

"State your business quickly. We're moving out," Logan said.

"Panmure, you're the son of the deceased Earl of Panmure. If you do not appear within a moon, you will forfeit your inheritance. You must appear before the magistrate, my lord."

Donnan blushed. Doing his best to hide his reaction, he forced out a response. "I'm sorry, I know not of what you speak. Clearly, this is a case of mistaken identity. Continue on, Ramsay."

Logan narrowed his gaze at Donnan, but he flicked the reins of his horse nevertheless. "Carry on, Torrian."

As they moved away, the man's calls followed them. "Thirty days until all of Cairnie Castle falls to your sire's enemy, my lord. Please do something. Your sister is desperate."

"Know you aught about this?" asked Torrian, who rode beside Donnan.

"Nay, I don't. Carry on."

"Cairnie Castle neighbors our land. I heard the old earl died around a moon ago. His daughter and her husband occupy the keep now, but they are to be sent out shortly. They have nowhere to go. Her brother disappeared several years ago," Logan explained to Torrian as he threw a covert glance over his shoulder at Donnan. "We've been waiting to see who will be awarded the land. I've already requested it for the Ramsays in case the new earl does not make his presence known."

Donnan gripped the reins of his horse, trying not to pass his tension on to the animal. The only two people who knew the truth of his situation were Quade and Logan Ramsay. He'd had to confess all before he was accepted into their clan because Logan had recognized him. He'd long since denounced his title and his position as heir, and he had no intention of changing his mind now.

Quade had informed him a fortnight ago about his sire's passing. The news had jarred him something fierce, but when the former laird had asked him to take his rightful place as the new earl and declare an alliance with the Ramsays, he'd refused.

He just couldn't do it. After the breach in his family, he could not bear to move back into Carnie Castle as if nothing had happened. His only regret was that he could not console his sister. This loss must have hit her hard. He would have to ensure that she and her husband inherited the castle, even if it required him to take the title in name.

"Donnan? Is everything all right? Is something wrong with your wound? Did you pop a stitch or two mayhap?" The concern in Bethia's voice warmed his heart. Even though she was undoubtedly still upset with him, Bethia Ramsay was a compassionate healer down to her core.

"Just a bit dizzy. I'll be fine in a moment." He forced himself to focus on the present and forget the past. He loved his sister, and someday he would return to visit with her, but not now.

As soon as he felt he'd mastered himself, he moved his horse up next to Bethia's mount. "My apologies for intruding on your thoughts, my lady, but may I ask a question?" Changing the subject was the best tactic.

Bethia kept her gaze focused directly in front of her. "Donnan, please do not do this. My name is Bethia, not my lady."

"Accepted. Bethia, may I ask you a question?"

"Answer me this question first and I will return the favor." She still refused to make eye contact.

"Aye, if you'll look at me." How he prayed she would not ask him the one question he could not answer...not here, not now. He'd never lie to her, but he would postpone the confrontation if he could. Telling her now, while they had an audience, could jeopardize all he'd been trying to build with her.

She turned her face to look at him, her expression devoid of all emotion.

He nodded. *One step at a time.* "My thanks. Now do we have an arrangement?"

She turned back to face forward, then said, "I agree. I'll start."

"Go ahead, I'm listening." How he hoped she wasn't about to ask him the one question he didn't wish to answer. He was not willing to be forthcoming about everything. Some things he preferred to forget.

"Do you know the Earl of Panmure?" She tipped her head toward him, he guessed to gauge his reaction.

He kept his horse at a steady gait, fighting the urge to gallop away. If only that foolish stranger hadn't planted ideas in everyone's heads. He thought for a quick moment and gave her an honest answer. "I knew the old Earl of Panmure. He could be a bit curmudgeonly, as he was advanced in age. Now may I ask my question?"

"Aye. I'll answer if I'm capable."

"My thanks." The partial moon had brought a memory back to him, and he was eager to know whether he had the right of it. "Before I was injured, I believe I saw Shewolf hit with an arrow. Do you know what happened to her?" His gaze scanned the area as he spoke.

"Aye. After I finished your stitches the first time, I washed my hands in the stream not far from where you were injured. Shewolf came to me, the arrow still in her side with the shaft broken off. I numbed the area with my salve and pulled it out, but I didn't dare stitch her."

Donnan was incredulous—even a wild beast had trusted the lass. "I would have held her for you. How bad was it?"

"Not bad. It wasn't verra deep. I managed to cover it with the same poultice I gave you in the hope of keeping the fever away."

"I appreciate you caring for my friend." His gaze carried over both sides of the land, searching for any sign of the beast.

"Donnan, I care about all animals, not just yours."

He gave her a sheepish look. "I know that. I didn't mean aught by it." He needed time alone with her, a chance to explain his feelings without an audience, but it was not to happen anytime soon. "I meant what I said about wishing to get to know you better."

"I feel the same, but…"

"But what?"

"But somehow everything changed in Edinburgh. I fear I have misjudged you. I feel I must sift through everything I know about you and find the true Donnan."

"I would like that," he replied. "Bethia, there are some truths I have yet to share with you, but this is not the place for such a discussion. I'd appreciate if you'd trust my judgment on this."

"Would it make me an innocent to trust you? That's the part that confuses me most. I fear I may be overly naïve and trusting." She paused for a moment. "Am I?"

"Nay, you are more intelligent than most, and wiser than many. Have faith in yourself. I promise to tell you all, but I'm not verra good with words. I need time to work through these things through on my own. I'm sorry, lass," he said, hanging his head, "I know that is not a verra good answer for you."

"But I sense 'tis an honest one. I also know you are still suffering from your injury. I would prefer that you have a clear mind when we have this conversation. As long as you promise to tell me everything in the near future, I accept it."

He nodded, but could he truly tell her *everything*?

If he did, he feared she'd hate him.

☾

Bearchun sat in the middle of the hut with his eyes closed. It was the only way he could be sure he wouldn't make the mistake of looking at his blood. He could not allow himself to faint in front of his new partner and the guards he'd hired for his last jaunt in the land of the Scots, so he kept his eyes squeezed shut and gritted his teeth, cursing on occasion as the old woman ran the needle through his skin and pulled it through.

"I agree with you," his partner said. "We must wait until we can sneak in without their knowledge. But I say all we need is the lass, the big one."

The words were said with delightful disdain. "Nay, I've told you 'tis not enough. I want the wee lassies too. I'll make that Jennet pay for what she cost me."

"Petty revenge is not going to help you. I say we get the lass, keep her until they pay us enough coin, and then leave her somewhere. They'll find her."

"You two are fools," one of the guards offered. "You could get prime coin for the lass if you sell her. There are plenty who'll buy a lass that young, especially an untouched one. You can double your coin—collect from Ramsay *and* from the dealer near the firth."

"If I do that, I'll not get to see the expression on Logan Ramsay's face. I want revenge—as petty as I can get it," Bearchun shouted.

"Calm yourself. Or did you forget they're here looking for you?" his new partner whispered. "If you cannot control yourself, you'll cost us everything. You agreed to wait until we have the upper hand."

Bearchun growled when the needle pierced his skin again. "Fine. We wait. But not too long. I want this finished as soon as they return."

In his mind, he thought of tying a wee lass to a tree and setting a mass of spiders free to crawl all over her body. He laughed. "I'll wait."

"I want wee Jennet."

***

They arrived back on Ramsay land early in the morning, before most people were awake. Donnan came to the stables to retrieve his dogs, then headed directly toward his cottage without another word.

Bethia dismounted with the help of her brother. She headed into the keep, eager to sleep and, if only for a while, forget the last two days. As soon as her head hit the pillow, she fell asleep.

Exhaustion only carried her so far. Four or five hours later, she awakened, her mind still in a turmoil over Donnan. She sat up in bed and rubbed her eyes. She needed to speak with three people, she decided: her mother; her father; and her sister, Lily.

Her parents needed to know what had transpired. She knew her uncle—he'd give her some time to explain all to her parents, but if she didn't, he would do it for her.

She had nothing to hide. Under no circumstances was she ashamed of her behavior. She would explain almost everything and see what their thoughts were on Donnan.

And Lily? Her sister had a way of explaining things better than anyone else. Lily wouldn't lie to her or offer her empty words. Some considered Lily simple; *her* description of her dear sister would be that Lily was simply brilliant.

Her first action upon climbing out of bed was to request a tub bath, something she knew would help her organize her thoughts. When all was ready, she settled down into the warm water and considered how best to approach her parents.

It wouldn't be with the heart of the matter—that she'd fallen in love with Donnan. Or was he Panmure? It was one of the many things she still didn't know about him.

When she considered her options carefully, she dried herself off and dressed, inhaling the scent of clean clothing with a sigh. How did men travel so much? It was downright odiferous. Giggling at her word choice, she wondered if it were real. If not, it should be.

When she entered the hall, she was surprised to see her mother and father were both still settled by the hearth. Her mother bolted out of her seat to greet her. "You are hale, daughter?"

"Aye, Mama." She gave her mother a kiss on the cheek and moved over to greet her sire the same way. "We got in so early, I did not wish to awaken you. I was desperately tired."

Her father didn't mince any words. "Brenna, please assist me into the solar. We need to talk, Bethia."

Bethia rolled her eyes. "Who approached you already? I had every intention of coming to you straight away. I was just over-tired."

Her mother patted her shoulder. "We know that, dearest. Uncle Logan just told your sire he needed to speak with you. He said naught more than that."

"I wish he would have waited. I did not wish to upset you."

Her father said, "He could not hold his peace. My brother and I have always been together. I'm used to his ways by now. If he was worried, he would have told me more. Should he have said more?"

"Nay, Papa. Come inside." Bethia's mama helped him out of his chair, and Bethia fell in beside him in case he needed someone to lean on. Her mother walked with them on the other side. "Your pain is back?"

"Nay, just a bad night. I've applied Jennie's poultice. It takes a wee bit of time for it to act."

Her mother looked past him to say, "Happens whenever he's worried about one of our children. He was worried about you."

"Papa, I'm a woman fully grown." She held the door of the solar open for him, and he stepped inside.

"I know that, but your mother and I have been overly protective of you, and I oft worried that 'twould cause you trouble someday. Lily and Torrian had traveled half the lands by the time they were your age, and Gregor has done the same by ten and six, but we always kept you at home. Has it caused you trouble?" He paused, leaning on his cane while he awaited her response. How she loved her sire. He always made difficult discussions so much easier than she feared they'd be.

How *unlike* Uncle Logan.

She patted his hand. "Nay, Papa. I wished to stay at home, but this was a verra different journey for me. Please sit down and I'll tell you all."

Once they settled, two expectant gazes settled on her from across her sire's desk and her sire reached over to hold her mama's hand, something he oft did. "Donnan had a terrible injury, and I will say your teachings served me well, Mama. I was able to stitch his wound, though I did have to repair the stitches."

"You stitched him twice? What happened? Did he fall and tear the first set?"

Her mother's expression told her Uncle Logan had indeed kept her secrets. "Mama, mayhap 'twould be easier if I just explain that I have developed feelings for Donnan. When I was alone with him to check his bandage, I kissed *him* and Uncle Logan caught us sitting verra close together behind a closed door. I'm sure 'tis what Uncle Logan wanted me to talk about with you. He was upset."

Her mother, who had been leaning so far forward that Bethia had feared she would topple over, leaned back and whispered, "Oh my."

Her father sat quietly as he oft did, giving careful consideration to his words before he spoke. "Allow me to fill in what happened next," he finally said. "Logan lost his temper before speaking to anyone, causing a scene that caused you to be thrown out of the inn."

Bethia couldn't help but smile. "Not quite, Papa. We were not thrown out, but 'twas quite a scene, and 'tis why Donnan's stitches needed to be repaired. Uncle Logan bellowed and swung his fists, Donnan fought back, and Torrian tried to stop it. Cailean and Sorcha were also involved. I ran outside crying. When I managed to control my tears, I came back inside to repair my stitchery, but not before I made all three men listen to my opinion, something they'd neglected to do before deciding Donnan and I were to marry immediately."

She waited for their reaction, and she was totally taken aback. The two looked at each other and burst out laughing.

Once they were capable of speaking, her mother said, "Good for you, daughter. You are twenty years old. You are quite capable of making your own decisions. 'Tis how we raised you, and both your grandmothers would be proud of you."

Her papa added, "Forget about Uncle Logan. He will come around. He's having a verra difficult time seeing all our wee lassies grow up and marry—Lily, Molly, Sorcha, and even Kyla. I suspect he thought you'd never be interested in a man, although I told him many times the day would come. He expected you'd stay the innocent forever. I told him 'twas time to move on to Lise and Liliana. In fact, when Jennet and Brigid marry, I suspect we'll need to tie him up again."

Her mother said, "What your papa is trying to tell you is that Uncle Logan only acted so boorishly because he adores you."

"I know. I recall him bellowing something about my innocence and sweetness being destroyed." She rolled her eyes, pleased her parents were reacting as they were.

It struck her that neither of them seemed surprised she was interested in Donnan. Her mother sat back and said, "Now, why don't you tell us about you and Donnan."

She couldn't contain her sigh, something her mother didn't miss, quirking her brow at her. "I'm verra confused. I have strong feelings for Donnan, but before we left for Edinburgh, he said he'd never marry again, that his first marriage 'twas too painful. Yet he does not push me away, instead pulling me closer whenever we're near." She held her hand up to her sire. "Papa, he's verra respectful, much more so than the younger lads."

"Henson?"

"Aye, Henson." She left it at that, not wishing to remind herself of the awful kiss he'd forced on her. "I like that Donnan is more mature, but I still have my doubts. I fear he's holding back." She explained the strange incident at the end of their journey, how someone had approached Donnan and called him the Earl of Panmure's heir.

As soon as she finished explaining everything, her mother came over and pulled her to her feet, wrapping her in a warm embrace. "If you'd like my advice…"

"Aye, I would. I feel I know naught about men and relationships."

"You need to have a private discussion with Donnan, and you need to ask him to be honest with you," she said.

Her father added, "And if he's not, *I* will be. Bethia, Donnan is a good man, but he has not told you all you need to know. Still, this isn't a conversation you should have in front of Logan either. If you'd like, I'll escort you out to his cottage and give you the chance to speak to him alone. He'll not be inappropriate with me just outside your door."

"I would like that, Papa."

"Then we'll go after the midday meal."

CHAPTER FOURTEEN

B EFORE BETHIA SPOKE WITH DONNAN, she needed to see her sister. She waited in the hall for Lily to enter with the twins, something she did everyday so they could share the midday meal with Kyle. She sighed with relief when Lily and Sorcha came in, each holding one of the twins. Och, how she adored the little ones.

"Come to Auntie Bethia," she held her arms out as they approached. Liliana reached for her with a giggle, so Bethia grabbed her and kissed her cheek. Sorcha unrolled the large blanket on the floor they kept in a basket near the hearth so the lassies could crawl around without getting stuck in the rushes.

"Bethia, I heard you had a most wonderful journey to Edinburgh," Lily said with a smirk. "I'm so glad you went along."

Bethia sat on a stool at the edge of the blanket, tossing a few toys out for the bairns to play with. She was so glad her mother and sister didn't believe in slinging bairns in plaids hanging on the wall for part of the day as some mothers did. It wasn't the Ramsay or Grant way.

Sorcha giggled. "I'll not forget it soon. Cailean loved having my sire's attention on someone else for a change."

"Tell me all about it," Lily said.

"Nay. Later," Bethia said. "People will be arriving soon and I must ask you an important question. Both of you. I'd like to hear your answers."

Lily stood up and pulled Bethia to her feet. "I've not heard you like this before. Go ahead. If 'tis important to you, then 'tis for me. You know how I love you, sister."

Bethia nodded, trying to keep from tearing up. Clearing her throat, she glanced at Sorcha, who gave her a nod of encouragement, then looked back to Lily. "I don't have much experience with men, and I do not wish to make an important decision out of naiveté."

"I'm listening," Lily said, holding her hands.

"How did you know? When did you know Kyle was the one for you? I've thought and thought, and I have no idea how I'm to know for sure."

Lily smiled. "You could not have asked me an easier question. There are two ways you can tell. The first is how you feel when he kisses you. If he makes you forget your name, then he's the one for you. Did Henson and his frog breath make you feel that way?"

Bethia laughed. "Nay. He made me wish to escape."

Lily's tone softened. "Did Donnan's kiss make you forget where you were?"

Her mind returned to how she'd felt in that chamber just before her uncle had banged open the door. "Aye." She'd forgotten *everything.* "And the second way?"

"If you feel different—nay, better—whenever he's near. Butterflies in your belly, losing yourself in the middle of a sentence, forgetting everything else but what's happening in the here and now."

The door opened and Kyle stepped inside, his gaze scanning the great hall before it settled on Lily. A broad smile stretched across his face, and Lily spun around and ran to him, shouting over her shoulder, "Sorcha, watch the twins."

Bethia looked at Sorcha and asked, "Did she do that intentionally? She forgot everything as soon as Kyle walked in."

Sorcha shook her head slowly. "She was just being honest. 'Tis exactly how it feels. 'Tis as if you are the only two people present. Do you feel that way about Donnan?"

She thought for a moment, considering it. Their relationship had been so unusual, and most of their interactions had involved her working as a healer—first on Wynda, then on Donnan. "I'm not sure."

Lily hurried back over to their spot in front of the hearth— flushed, smiling, and deliriously happy because Kyle was behind her. "You see? It still happens to me."

Kyle bent over, scooped Lise up, and tossed her into the air until she erupted in a squeal of giggles.

A group of lasses came inside, all of them giggling and whispering. Sorcha asked, "What do you suppose they're whispering about?"

Pieces of their conversations reached their ears.

"...like me..."

"I want him."

"What happened?"

"...be mine..."

"...so handsome..."

"Who are they talking about?" Lily whispered.

"I'm not sure," Sorcha said. "I didn't hear any names, just that they sure do like him."

Lily squeezed Bethia's hand and said, "Trust me. When it happens, you'll know."

She picked up Liliana and held her out to Bethia, who reached for her—then froze when the door opened again.

Donnan stood there. Her hands immediately dropped to her side.

If it were even possible, he was more handsome than he'd been in Edinburgh. It was painfully obvious that those lasses had been talking about *him*. His gaze searched the area, but the lasses practically charged at him, asking him a multitude of questions. Rather than pay them any mind, he continued to search the hall, not stopping until his gaze caught hers. He headed directly toward her, and Bethia's belly did that flopping thing again while her body overheated, causing her hands to sweat.

Lily interrupted her thoughts by kissing her cheek and whispering in her ear, "I think you know *exactly* what I mean. My guess is he's the one. I'm happy for you."

Bethia jerked toward Lily, feeling as if she'd just been jarred awake from a very pleasant dream. "Oh, forgive me. You wished me to take Liliana. I can take her."

"Nay," her sister replied with a smile. "You have more important things to tend to at the moment. The lasses are right—he looks quite different with his hair trimmed and cleanly shaven."

When she shifted her gaze back to Donnan, he had nearly reached her. The lasses were staring at them with sour looks on their faces, but she ignored them as he came to a halt in front of her and said, "Good day to you, Bethia. Is your sire available?"

Bethia lost all ability to speak. He even smelled fresh, like the pine trees and the wind blowing through the trees. Her sister saved her.

"Greetings, Donnan. I heard you were injured. Are you feeling better?"

"Aye. Thanks to your sister's skills, I am much better." Liliana sat on her mother's hip. Her expression had turned quite serious as she stared at this new stranger, her wee brow furrowing and her bottom lip protruding.

Donnan peered at Liliana. "Your daughter is a beauty, Lily."

"Thank you." Lily's gaze didn't miss much, checking him over so thoroughly it was almost embarrassing.

Donnan rubbed the back of his hand across the wee one's cheek. His voice changed completely to a soft, warm tone. "But I think this bairn knows how charming she is, do you not, my sweet?" He smiled and Liliana giggled, instantly accepting him as a friend.

Bethia's heart melted.

"Would you like to hold her, Donnan?" Lily asked.

"I would love to, but…"

Kyle said, "Lily, the man just took a sword wound to his belly. He'll not be lifting aught, or his healer—" he tipped his head toward Bethia, "—will refuse to ever treat him again."

"True, verra true," Donnan said, shuffling his feet. "Mayhap another time."

"Lily, I'd like to eat now, if you do not mind," Kyle said. "'Twas a busy morn in the lists. The girls can eat with us." They headed toward the trestle tables in the middle of the hall.

Sorcha winked at Bethia behind Donnan's back as she went to the door to greet Cailean.

They were alone.

"Donnan, I know my sire would be happy to speak with you. In fact, he offered to bring me to your cottage after the meal. But I'd like to speak to you alone first, if you please."

He quirked his brow at her. "Will that be allowed? I'd prefer to do everything properly."

Bethia's mother appeared out of nowhere, cupping her elbow from behind and saying, "Greetings to you, Donnan. Would you two like to talk in the solar? We'll leave the door open so there'll be no impropriety. I'll be seated over there near the hearth, where I can see you. Not that I do not trust the two of you, but I know how others talk."

Bethia glanced at Donnan, waiting to hear his response.

"Aye," he said, though a strange look crossed his face. "I do need to speak with you and allow you the opportunity to ask the questions you spoke of on the journey back from Edinburgh."

She nodded and headed into the solar, Donnan following her. She couldn't help but notice all the gazes that followed them into the chamber off the hall. Her cheeks burned, and she knew without looking they were flushed.

Once inside, she sat in the chair across from her sire's desk and he settled in the one beside her. "Please allow me to start. I've given this much thought, and I believe you need to be aware of everything. I hadn't wished to confess all, but you deserve to know the full truth."

Bethia was pleased with this declaration so she folded her hands in her lap, indicating she was ready to listen.

He lifted his gaze to hers and she was lost. There was so much pain in his eyes that it simply broke her heart.

"Bethia, I did not just know the former Earl of Panmure—he was my sire." He glanced up to see her reaction, but she did her best not to show one. She needed to hear the entire story before she cast judgment.

"Five years ago, I fell in love with a lass unlike any I'd ever met before. Or I should say that I thought I loved her. I met Glenna at court that season. She was quite beautiful, and…" He paused, squeezing his eyes shut for a moment before he continued. "I know not how else to say this, but I was an impressionable young man, and she bewitched me with her talents in the bed chamber. She'd set her sights on me, and I succumbed without much thought.

"My sire called her some verra unkind names. She was a beautiful woman, but he believed her heart was black. I argued with him, but to no avail. He had hoped to marry me to a lass of noble blood." He sighed and ran a hand through his newly shorn hair. "He'd actually planned to talk with your sire and another laird near the borderland. He begged me to reconsider, threatening to cut me off from my inheritance if I continued my relationship with Glenna.

"I believed in love, and I believed in Glenna, though it proved to be one of my biggest mistakes. Glenna and I found a priest to marry us, and I'd never been so happy."

He paused to lean forward, resting his elbows on his knees with his hands clasped in front of him. "My family owns two properties: Cairnie Castle and a small cottage outside of Edinburgh. 'Twas built as a hunting cottage and rarely used by the family. My sire refused to allow us into Cairnie Castle, so I had no choice but to bring my new wife to the cottage.

"The day we arrived outside the cottage was the day Glenna's lies started to unravel. When she saw the cottage, she was furious, wondering where her servants were and what her new title would be. I explained that we'd given it all up because my sire didn't support the marriage. She truly believed there was some law that could force my sire to give us the castle."

He tipped his head with a smile. "I explained to her that she didn't know my sire verra well."

"Donnan, forgive me for interrupting, but that man in Edinburgh mentioned something about a sister…"

"Och, aye. I had a brother who was older than me who died when he fell from a horse. I still have a sister, married, and she was living with my sire the last I knew. But she could not inherit the castle if there is a living male. I would have thought my father would have changed his inheritance so that Cairnie Castle would go to her, but apparently he did not. I love my sister, and she married a wonderful man. I've not seen her in years."

He sat back up before he continued. "We lived in the cottage for about a year before it became clear that we could not support ourselves there. I'd set some coin aside, but it dwindled quickly, especially with all the gowns Glenna ordered for her wardrobe.

"Eventually, we were forced to move away. I'd met your uncle, and he was aware of my circumstances. He invited us to Ramsay land and promised not to tell anyone other than your sire of my past. I did not want anyone knowing my true name."

"What is your true name?"

"Donnan Douglas, who would have been the future Earl of Panmure living in Cairnie Castle had it not been for his foolish besotted behavior over Glenna. Now I recognize how wrong my actions were, but 'twas too late.'"

"Why? I would go to a hunting cottage with you if we were in love. I don't believe it should matter where you live." She would follow him anywhere if she was sure of their love.

"Aye, I believe you mean that. However, Glenna would not agree with you. We moved to Ramsay land and she discovered she was carrying our child. We had moved into one of the only available huts at the time, which happened to be about a third of the size of my sire's hunting cottage. She was not happy, but she had a difficult pregnancy, so she was oft abed. At one point, she confessed that she'd married me because she wanted to be a countess with servants to tend to her needs. She wished for me to go back and beg forgiveness from my father, but I refused."

"Why?"

"Because my father was the most stubborn man of all, and I have gained much of his stubbornness. Neither of us would give in to the other. I was certain of that, but she would not let it go.

"Then our son was born, and I hoped it would help us repair our marriage and build our family. She found wee Donnie dead less than a moon later. She was never happy after that, and it did not surprise me when she left me for another."

Bethia considered all he'd told her.

"I told you I would answer any questions you have, so I'm willing to do that now. What else do you wish to ask me?" He sat up and waited for her questions.

"Did you know your father had died?"

He stared at his hands, rubbing one on top of the other. "Aye. Your papa had already informed me of the news."

"Do you regret that you never saw your father again?"

"Aye, I do," he said, still rubbing his hands together. Then he looked up at her with his sad gray eyes. "But my first reaction was that he'd gotten his wish. The last thing he ever said to me was that he never wanted to see me again."

"Oh, Donnan. I'm so sorry he sent you away like that. You have my sympathies."

"My thanks, but I have learned to accept it. Despite the way our relationship ended, I believe he truly did love me as his son."

Bethia thought about her wonderful, close relationship with her parents. How would she go on if she ever lost their love, their approval? "He taught you your love of working with your hands, did he not?"

"Aye. He taught me how to fell a tree—and how to cut it into the best wood. He built small pieces of furniture with me. Those are my favorite memories of my sire, not the ones when he was in full dress. His title always made him seem unapproachable, *unreasonable*, but he was anything but in my younger days."

"And your mother?"

"She died within a year of giving birth to my sister. I don't remember her. I think 'twas devastating to my sire, if I had to guess, although he did not talk about it often."

Their conversation brought new clarity to Donnan's evasiveness yesterday. How did one admit to severing a relationship with a parent, to choosing a woman over one's family, especially since Donnan clearly recognized his mistake? While she had many more questions, she decided she'd caused him enough pain for one day.

"I only have one more question." One persistent question that she wished to ignore but could not.

"Go ahead. I'll answer if I'm able."

"Are you not still married to Glenna? How could you consider a relationship with me if you are still married to your wife?"

CHAPTER FIFTEEN

D ONNAN WAS TAKEN ABACK BY Bethia's boldness, yet he was secretly pleased. He'd prefer a woman who spoke her mind to one who kept secrets and had hidden agendas.

There would be no hidden agendas with Bethia Ramsay.

"I've considered that ever since we met, though only briefly at first. Every day I spend with you, I wonder more about it. My intention is to end the marriage by desertion. I may need to place a petition with King Alexander."

"She did desert you, correct?"

"Aye. A few months after we lost our son, she told me she'd found another. Said she was unhappy in the Highlands because it was so desolate. I wished her happiness and have not seen her since."

He chuckled. "I also reminded her that Ramsay land, being in West Lothian, is just on the edge of the Highlands, but all she did was curse at me about how isolated we were. Something about new gowns and ribbons…" He waved his hand, indicating he wasn't interested in his wife's greedy desires for objects and gems.

"Will you return to Edinburgh now that you know your sire is dead?"

He smirked. "I guess you had more than one question, aye? I do not mind answering." He took a deep breath before he continued. "I don't have any desire to take over Cairnie Castle, but my sister deserves to live there with her husband. I'll likely have to claim my title in order for that to happen. I'll speak to your sire about how to best approach the matter. I'm not sure if I'm quite ready to travel back to Edinburgh yet. At the moment, I'm more interested in making a particular woman happy." He glanced at her, eager to see how she would react to that declaration.

He had learned the hard way what mattered in life. Objects, gowns, castles, jewels…they didn't matter. They couldn't make one happy. Working with his hands gave him much more satisfaction than anything else he'd ever done, other than becoming a sire to wee Donnie. Those two things had given him a sense of worthiness, not the objects others like Glenna desired.

"Donnan, I don't know what to say. 'Tis such a sweet thought."

He stood up and said, "I meant what I said in Edinburgh. I'd like to ask your sire for your hand if you'll have me."

"Why have you changed? You told me before you'd never marry again."

Hell, but the lass was beautiful, intelligent, curious, and caring, and…what more could he want? More than anything, he wished to make her happy. To be the kind of man who was deserving of her love. How could he explain that?

"Quite simply because being around you makes me happier than I've ever been. You are inspiring, and you make me wish to be a better person. You won't accept mediocrity or laziness from me. I need you in my life. I think we could be happy anywhere. But know this…"

"What?" she asked on a gasp.

This was hardest for him to admit, but it came from his heart. "If 'twould make you happier for me to step out of your life, I would do it. Just say the word, and I'll drop my suit."

He waited, almost afraid to hear her answer, though there was no denying what had transpired between them in Edinburgh. They had a connection. She was a passionate woman, and he would give away ten castles to be the man who showed her what to do with that drive.

Still, he meant what he'd said. If she denied him, he'd walk away even though his heart would be broken.

"I will not deny you, Donnan. I would like to get to know you better. That is where I stand at the moment. You may talk to my sire if it would please you, but I cannot accept or deny your proposal at this time."

He smiled and stepped closer, giving her a chaste kiss on her lips before they were interrupted.

Her sire stood in the doorway.

Donnan stepped away from Bethia to greet her sire. "Greetings, my laird. May I have a moment of your time?"

"I have the time. I'll ask my daughter if she minds our conversation?"

"Nay, Papa. Donnan did propose marriage to me, and I told him I'm not ready yet, but that I would like to get to know him better. He also informed me of his true heritage as the future Earl of Panmure."

Another face appeared in the door. "Good, because I'd like to speak to him about that." Uncle Logan stood in the doorway.

Bethia crossed her arms in front of her. "And what else do you wish to speak to him about, Uncle?"

"Bethia, I've apologized to you already, but beware, Douglas. If you attempt to take the sweetness from my dear niece, you'll have to answer to me."

Bethia rolled her eyes and whispered, "Poor Brigid." With that, she kissed her uncle's cheek and left.

Donnan watched her leave with regret. He knew her sire would ask him if he'd been honest about everything. He hadn't been.

He'd told her almost everything about his past, but he couldn't tell her the one thing that hovered over every day—nay, every moment—of his life.

He couldn't tell her when there were so many outside the door. She'd either scream or cry.

He had no idea which one.

❧

The following morn, Bethia skirted around the field one more time. Today was one of her brother Torrian's favorite days—the dog races. Her father and brother had carried on a long discussion about canceling or postponing the yearly event because the races took place outside the gates, but Torrian, Logan, and Kyle had convinced her sire that they could make it safe. They would keep everyone in a small area surrounded by guards. Torrian would not be denied this event, though many of his guards would have to listen at a distance instead of attend the races directly.

Logan thought the festival could actually draw Bearchun out, so they decided to hold it in the evening, as usual, with the goal of setting a trap for the fool.

Though she would prefer to stay as far away from Bearchun as possible, Bethia was grateful the event hadn't been cancelled. In truth, it was one of her favorites as well.

Ever since his dear friend, Growley, had helped him learn how to walk again after his long illness, Torrian had raised and bred Deerhounds, the breed of dogs most loved by the Scots. He loved to deliver new pups to his friends, even giving some to the Grants—people he trusted to treat them well. It was well known that if anyone ever mistreated one of Torrian's dogs, Torrian would collect the dog and never allow that person another pet.

Wiry, gray hair covered many of his beloved hounds, but red, brown, and white coats were often seen as well. Other dogs were also allowed to compete, and they did so based on their size. Bethia liked watching the deerhounds best because of their long strides. They were quite simply beautiful when in their element, running as hounds were meant to do.

Torrian had always been impressed with how intelligent and perceptive his dear Growley had been. The dog had always been his friend and companion, someone he could rely on to help and support him. This event, a series of racing competitions, was about thanking the dogs. He and Kyle had already hunted a boar and a deer, and special bones would go to the winners of the event, while the clan would feast on the deer meat at the end of the day's festivities.

Bethia brought the new pups with her and found a spot near the race path to settle. She sat on a plaid against the chill and settled the pups in an area around her. It wasn't long before a gaggle of bairns ran to join her, all begging to play with the pups.

She'd left Bretta back at the stables so she wouldn't be upset by the attention the pups would receive. They were over a fortnight old, so she'd decided to bring them out to see how they fared with others. Lily came running over with Maggie, each of them carrying a squealing twin. They set the wee lassies down a short distance away, and they immediately crawled into Bethia's lap. They started pushing each other in an attempt to take a wee bit more of Bethia's lap.

Lily and Maggie sat down on either side of her with two perfectly timed huffs. "Bethia, did you hear what our uncle is doing?"

Lily asked.

"Nay, what?"

"He's decided to hold a contest for Queen of the Festival."

Bethia couldn't believe what she'd heard. "Uncle Logan?" She reached over to grab two pups and settled them in the twins' laps, much to their delight.

"Aye. Since when does Uncle Logan look at a woman's beauty? He believes the most beautiful women are the ones who can fire an arrow like Aunt Gwyneth."

"I agree," Bethia said, glancing at Maggie. "We all recall how he reacted to the knowledge that you are so skilled with a dagger. What are the qualifications?"

Lily shook her head, apparently still amazed at their uncle. "I heard him say, 'the most beautiful unmarried Ramsay lass,' to one, but then he said, 'the most beautiful soul,' to another. What do you suppose this is really about?"

Maggie said, "You never know with my sire." She played with another one of the pups, giggling.

Bethia rolled her eyes, then grabbed one of the twin's hands. Liliana had managed to grab her pup's tail. "One never knows with Uncle Logan, but he has an ulterior motive. We all know it. Mayhap he wants Maggie to win."

Maggie jerked her head up. "Nay, not me. He knows I'll not accept it."

Lily pondered before she answered, "Mayhap you're right. But he does adore you, Maggie. Could be he wishes to give you the opportunity to show off your special prowess." Lily grinned as she said it, and Bethia couldn't help but smile too.

They were interrupted by Torrian. "Bethia, you'll stay through most of the races in case we have any injuries?"

"Of course, Torrian. I'll not be far." Lise and Liliana giggled as Torrian bent over to plant a kiss on each one's cheek. He made a point of petting each of the pups. He always made sure to treat each animal the same. No one was kinder to animals than her dear brother.

Or so she'd thought until she met Donnan.

He laughed. "I'm sure you will not be allowed to leave." His hand pointed off to the distance. "More of your admirers are coming."

Bethia turned her head to see her sister, Jennet, and her cousin, Brigid, come pouncing toward them, landing on the ground beside them in a heap of giggles. Brigid giggled uncontrollably, which sent Lise and Liliana both into giggles.

"They all love you, Bethia," Lily announced, leaning back on her elbows in the grass. "We all do."

Bethia found her gaze drifting to the side of the meadow. Donnan stood alone with his dogs, all three settled at his feet. His gaze caught hers and she smiled.

Lily followed her gaze and whispered, "I like the two of you together. Who knew what a handsome man was hidden behind all that hair? Verra handsome." She leaned over to whisper in her ear. "Look at all the lassies making their way over to him."

Bethia did her best to ignore Donnan's entourage, focusing instead on the four lassies around her. Jennet and Brigid stood and began to chase the puppies around, much to the glee of the twins, who crawled out of Bethia's lap so they too could try to catch the puppies.

Kyle and Torrian gave directions to all those who had animals racing in the festivities, starting with the smallest dogs. Once they were all lined up, Kyle waved a flag and the dogs took off to a roar from the crowd and barking from the dogs waiting to race.

A short time later, three lasses, all nearly of age to marry, made their way over to Bethia.

The apparent leader of the group, Colina, asked, "Bethia, have you heard about the new contest, Queen of the Festival?"

"Aye, I've heard of it, but I don't know much about it." She had to admit her curiosity was piqued. She was not friends with any of them. They were shallow and downright mean at times. These were some of the lasses who'd spoken badly of her and Donnan at the party her parents had held for her.

The girls waited until Jennet, Brigid, Maggie, and Lily were out of hearing distance before they spoke. All of them were running about with the twins and the puppies.

Gormal, a homely girl with muddy brown hair, said, "So are you allowed to enter?" Her friend Mor stood behind her, apparently hiding, though Bethia wasn't sure why.

"I'm sure she would not be," Colina replied. "She's part of the laird's family, so it would not be fair for her to enter, would it,

Bethia?" She flashed a phony smile, showing her white teeth.

While Gormal was homely, Colina was a beauty with a lovely smile, blue eyes, and flowing red hair. Her heart was as black as Bearchun's, or so it seemed. Bethia did her best to avoid her. The lass was downright sneaky in all she did.

"I'm not interested in entering any type of contest, so do not worry, Colina." She picked up one of the pups, who struggled to follow the rest of the litter into the deep grasses.

"Worried?" Colina pursed her lips and planted a hand on one hip. "I'm not worried about any of my competition, just as I'm not worried about anyone stealing Donnan away from me."

Bethia had a difficult time containing her shock. "Donnan? If I recall, the first time you saw him, you said he reminded you of a recluse who belonged in the caves. Was that not how I heard it?"

Colina tilted her chin, her haughtiness obvious to everyone. "Mayhap I said so when he was hairy, but shaven, I like him. We just had a lovely conversation and he invited me to dine with him in the keep this eve after the festivities are moved inside. Was that not thoughtful of him?" She turned around to wave at Donnan, but he ignored her, instead staring into Bethia's eyes, a look that shot straight to her core.

Hell, but he was an intense man.

She wondered why he would wish to dine with Colina. They did not seem to suit each other at all, and he'd made it very clear he was interested in Bethia.

Torrian's voice interrupted them. "Bethia, will you check the dog with the white fur, please?"

She got to her feet and moved toward the wailing dog, but not before Colina whispered to her two friends. "I do not think I've ever seen anyone have such difficulty standing up. She is quite large, is she not?"

Gormal whispered something back, but only one word stood out: "Chubby."

Bethia froze and turned around just in time to see Lily take a tumble and fall directly on Colina with a just changed soiled rag-gie in her hand. "Oh dear, do forgive me, Colina."

Colina squealed, pushing Lily away from her and checking her gown. "Look what you did, you silly fool." As if just realizing what she'd said to the laird's sister, she stared at Lily with a wide-eyed expression. "Sorry, Lady Lily." Colina looked around nervously, probably to see if Kyle had overheard. His fierce protectiveness of his wife was legendary in the clan. Much to her obvious horror, Kyle *had* heard, and his eyes were ablaze with fury. Bethia would have laughed, but his expression was actually terrifying.

Kyle was at Lily's side in an instant, Jennet and Brigid watching the twins. "Did you just insult my wife?"

"Nay, I did not mean... Sorry..." She spun on her heal and ran off, Gormal and Mor following her.

"My thanks, Kyle." Lily kissed him.

"That lass," he shook his head. "I'm going to talk with her mother. I don't take kindly to her attitude."

"I could have handled the situation," Lily said, giving him her sweetest smile.

"I know. I saw you start to handle her, 'tis why I came over so quickly. True, she had a little pish coming, but I feared you wouldn't stop there. I know what you would do to defend your sister." He walked away, his hands on his hips, but peered back over his shoulder and asked, "I have faith you made a direct hit, wife?"

Lily wrinkled her nose and nodded. "Just a wee bit, but 'twas enough."

Bethia spun on her heel and headed over to the whining ball of fur off to the side of the track. How much worse could things get? It had been embarrassing enough when they'd insulted her at her party, now they'd insulted her to her face, and involved her sister and Kyle. The color on her face could not be any darker as she hustled over to the struggling animal.

Fortunately, it was an animal she'd treated before, so she sat on the ground to allow the wee beast to come to her. After one more pained circle, the dog finally ran over to her and fell sideways across her lap. She'd assessed his limping, so she settled the dog on his back and held the injured paw up to her eye while the dog finally ceased his yelping.

After careful consideration, she said, "'Tis just a wee nettle in your paw." She removed the offending agent and the dog jumped off her lap, running in a circle as if to test his paw, then ran back to Bethia to lick her cheek. Laughing, she waved the dog away just as a hand bronzed by the sun reached down to help her to stand. She allowed the assistance and stood, only to find herself staring straight into Donnan's eyes.

"What did she say to you?"

"Donnan, it does not matter to me. I care not what Colina says."

"But I do," he whispered. "I could see it in your countenance as soon as the nasty words left her mouth. You recovered well, but her barb hurt you."

Tears misted her eyes at the fact that he'd noticed all those things from a distance. "It does not matter, and I will not dignify her remark by repeating it." She sighed and pinched her eyes closed to stop the tears from flooding her cheeks. "I accept who I am."

"I hope so. What matters is your intelligence and your compassion, not your size, but you should know that I prefer a woman closer to my size. I always wondered why some men preferred wee lassies. I'd be afraid they could break. I like a woman who can fill my hands. Your curves would fit me perfectly."

She blushed, pleased by his words. "I hear you invited her to dine with you."

"Truly? 'Tis a lie. She invited me, but I rejected her. I have eyes for no one but you."

She turned away, unsure of how to respond to his intimate compliments but enjoying them just the same.

He followed her and said, "Forgive me, Lady Bethia. I did not intend to upset you. Mayhap I was too blunt. I've not been around many women of late."

She pivoted to face him and said, "You did not upset me, but I'm still a wee bit confused. This is all so new to me."

He whispered, "I am interested in you, verra interested. Bethia."

She noticed his gaze traveling over her shoulder, so she glanced in that direction to see what drew his attention. "What is it?"

"Saints preserve me, I hope my eyes are deceiving me." He reached for her hand and squeezed it before he let go. "I must go. Forgive me, but I'll find you later."

She didn't like the pained expression on his face one bit. "Who is it?"

In a voice only she could hear, he replied, "My wife."

CHAPTER SIXTEEN

DONNAN HURRIED BACK TOWARD THE gates, grateful they were a distance away from the festivities. Sure enough, there was Glenna atop her horse with two men on horseback riding behind her, raising a small ruckus with the guards at the gate.

"Nay, you'll not gain entrance. Mayhap you did used to be part of the Clan Ramsay, but I do not recall who you are." Cailean MacAdam had been given the duty of guarding the keep during the races, a fine time to distract the guards.

"Then we'll go to the festivities and I'll find someone to vouch for me." His wife's voice carried to him over the din.

"Nay, you won't. Not while I'm here. I doubt your small horse can outrun my stallion." Cailean's horse pranced a bit, as if to show off for his master.

"I want you to find my husband now." She crossed her arms and stared at MacAdam as if her looks alone would affect him.

He snorted, basically ignoring her.

"Find him now, I say," she sneered, raising her voice.

"Who is he? Then mayhap I'll think about it." Two other guards stood behind Cailean, while three were on top of the curtain wall, arrows already set to fire.

"My husband is Donnan Douglas, the new Earl of Panmure. Are you so ignorant?"

Cailean guided his destrier around her small mount. "I'd watch your tone if I were you, lady, or my mount will be eating yours for dinner. Take your men off Ramsay land. We're not impressed with your bluster."

"Why, I have never been so insulted! I'll tell your laird how rude you've been…"

Donnan had heard enough. Shouting over the noise from the fields, he said, "Glenna, enough. Dismount, and I'll speak with you over there." He pointed to a copse of trees outside of the gates. "Since you left me, 'tis all I'll give you. A quarter of an hour, and then I'll send you on your way."

One of her guards dismounted and rushed over to assist her down from her horse. Once she landed on her feet, she shoved the guard away and settled her hair and her brat, spinning on her heel to face him.

"How dare you insult me in front of lowly guards." Her hands went to her hips, and Donnan knew exactly what would come next. She was still magnificently beautiful, but her black heart changed everything. "You have no respect for me, you never have…"

He interrupted her, not willing to give any attention to her well-practiced attention-seeking behavior. He set his hand on the small of her back and pushed her over to the side. "Hurry, or I'll leave you here."

MacAdam yelled out, "I'd be happy to send her off, Donnan."

Glenna shouted at him, "That guard is rude. You need to speak to Quade about him and have him banished. Does he not know who I am?"

"Nay, he does not, and that guard is Logan Ramsay's son-in-law, so you'll get nowhere with your misguided demands. He's the best guard we have, in Logan's opinion."

She glared at him, but they'd finally reached the group of trees where they'd not be in the way of anyone on horseback. All of a sudden, her entire demeanor changed. "Donnan, 'tis so wonderful to finally see you again. I've been searching for you, but I've failed so many times."

Glenna attempted to throw her arms around his neck, but he ducked her embrace, and gently pushed her away from him. "Glenna, do not treat me like a fool. You left me, if you do not recall, and I have been on Ramsay land ever since, much happier, by the way. I'd prefer it if you'd marry another and set me free."

She smiled that expression he knew well—a crafty expression that spoke of her deceit. "Have you not missed me, dear husband? I've missed you."

"Nay, I have not missed you. What do you want? End the small talk." He gave her a piercing look, hoping she'd take the hint. She'd deserted *him*.

Glenna positioned herself closer to him, a strategic move on her part, but he recognized it as an attempted seduction. He would not be brought under her spell again. "I want the same thing I've always wanted. I want the coin that allows me to do whatever I want, and buy whatever I want."

"I don't have much coin. You know that, so why are you here?" He knew the answer, but he would force her to say it.

"Have you not heard that your own dear father has passed on?"

"I have heard."

"Then why have you not gone to claim your rightful place as his heir? You are now the Earl of Panmure."

"If I choose to be, I could be the Earl of Panmure. I am neither interested in my sire's castle nor his title. Have you forgotten that he disinherited me when I married you?"

She moved a step closer to him, her eyes turning into that beady, intense stare he hated. This was a woman set on getting what she wanted.

How different she was from dear Bethia.

"I have not forgotten, but you are his only heir, so you know the courts will ignore his foolishness and grant you his title. There is no one else."

"I do not want his title. I prefer a simple life."

"You will claim your inheritance, and I will return as your wife."

He chuckled. "I just told you I'm not interested. I may have been young and foolish enough to fall prey to your manipulations before, but no longer."

"Why not? Are you slipping your cock into another? Fine. Bring her along, and you can keep slipping it into her. I care not. You were a terrible lover."

"Nay. Go back to the rock you slithered out from under." He spun on his heel and strode away.

"I've told you before. I wish to be a countess—'tis the reason I married you. If you do not do as I wish, I'll tell all and you'll be hanged."

He spun back around, anger blackening his heart to match hers. "You'll tell what? That I loved our son and you didn't? That you left me because I wouldn't take you to Edinburgh to buy you new gowns every day? That you were the worst mother in the world, hating your own flesh and blood?" He knew the last part had come out in a bellow, but he did not care. The fury inside him could not be tamed. Glenna's deceit and callousness knew no bounds.

Glenna snickered. "That could all be true, but there is no law against any of it. Your actions were far worse than mine."

"And what exactly is it you are threatening me with?"

"Either you return to claim your inheritance and claim me as your wife, or I'll go to our king and tell him the truth." She crossed her arms, a slow grin spreading across her face.

"What truth?" But he already knew the answer. He knew what vileness she was about to spew.

"Do as I say, or I'll tell him how you killed our son."

Donnan fisted his hands, stepping back because he feared he would hit her.

She continued, her eyes full of satisfaction. "You have two days to think on it before I return, or I'll tell everyone the truth, murderer."

❦

Bethia returned to her spot, her gaze on Donnan. He was leaving, and he wasn't moving slowly.

She couldn't tear her gaze from what drew him. A woman stood at the gates, attempting to gain entrance to their castle.

Was it truly his wife?

The lump that formed in Bethia's throat threatened to choke her. She moved as if in a trance, heading slowly in their direction.

The closer she came, the more she could see the woman. She dismounted and stood in front of Donnan, a serious expression on her face. Her gown underneath her brat was beautiful, a dark red that accentuated her tiny waist and curves. Her lovely face was made almost ugly by an expression of fury. The two of them marched over to a group of trees not far from where she stood, oblivious to everyone around them.

Though she told herself to stop, she couldn't. One foot stepped in front of the other, not stopping until she was close enough to overhear their conversation, though bits and pieces fell out.

Glenna was trying to force Donnan to accept his inheritance.

The title and the riches were all she'd ever wanted. Her conversation moved along, but Bethia's mind was stuck on one small detail. This woman was his wife.

How could Donnan and Bethia ever marry if his wife wished to have him back?

Her mind raced through all kinds of conjectures, of how she'd probably just lost the one man who'd ever desired her and treated her with the respect she deserved. She'd lost the one chance she'd ever had for love.

What she heard next caused her to lose all sense of reason, something she couldn't even begin to understand.

His wife had accused him of killing their son. Killing. She'd called him a murderer, threatened to inform their king.

If it were true, Donnan would be hanged.

Could it be true?

Her mother would have known, wouldn't she have? She scrambled to recall her mother's exact words about the bairn's death. He'd died in his sleep. That was exactly what she'd said, the bairn had fallen asleep and never awakened.

How could that be considered murder?

Was his wife telling the truth or fabricating something for her own benefit?

Something inside Bethia shattered and she started running, searching for an area where she could be alone. She ran and ran, tears flooding her cheeks until she could not see anything in front of her. She wished to run away from Donnan's beautiful wife and her nasty accusations.

She couldn't believe it of him—she just couldn't.

Her feet carried her deeper into the forest until a pair of arms grabbed her from behind. She screamed, only one word on her mind.

Bearchun.

CHAPTER SEVENTEEN

ᔕ

DONNAN GRABBED HER FROM BEHIND, sick that she'd overheard his conniving wife. Bethia turned around and shoved against his chest. "Leave me be. Unhand me, you brute!"

"Bethia, it's me. I'm sorry. Please allow me to explain."

She shoved him again, but the effort was only half-hearted this time. "Did you truly murder your own son?"

"Bethia, listen to me."

She squirmed and struggled against him, so upset that she was unable to listen to reason, but he wouldn't let her go, not until she allowed him the chance to explain.

"Bethia, 'twas an accident. An accident."

Her gaze caught his and the look in her eyes wrenched his heart.

"An accident." He had to make her understand. "I did not do it apurpose."

"What? What are you saying?" Her tears slowed, and her breath hitched in response to his declaration.

"Sweet, will you listen? Allow me to explain. Please, I beg you. I'll not survive if you believe something so horrible of me."

Nodding, she gripped his forearms. "I'm listening." She gulped and gazed up at him.

He rubbed his thumbs across her arms. "I took him to bed with me. He was crying because his belly ached, I think. Glenna put him in his cradle, and he screamed so, I could not bear it. I picked him up and held him close, hoping my body heat would soothe him. He fell asleep, and so did I. When Glenna awakened me a few hours later, she was screaming that he was dead. And he was…dead in my arms. But I know not how he died. Your mother came to see him and said bairns just die in their sleep sometimes. But Glenna? She told your mother over and over again that I had rolled over him in my sleep and suffocated him."

Bethia's hand went straight to her mouth. "Oh, Donnan. How horrible."

"If she wishes to make trouble, she will."

A voice from behind him interrupted them.

"So you are slipping your cock into a sweet lassie. Is she not a chunky one?" Glenna stood not far from them, a wide smile on her face.

"Do not talk of her that way, Glenna. This is Quade and Brenna's daughter and you will not disrespect her. We have not had relations."

"Yet. As I said, Donnan, you may keep her. This is even better. Now I have something more to hold over your head."

He turned around to face her. "I knew your heart was black, but this is low even for you. I'll take my inheritance and gift you with all the coin you need to stay away from me. This marriage is over in my eyes. You are a conspiring, scheming wastrel. Leave now. I'll get your coin when I travel to Cairnie Castle. Come to see me in three days and I'll arrange for your funds, but only under the condition that you stay away from me. You cannot desert me and return whenever you have a whim. I intend to dissolve this marriage by desertion. I'll petition King Alexander. Do you hear me, Glenna?"

She came closer to him and said, "Dig deep, husband. I'll be needing a large sum to support me for the rest of my days. I doubt you'll find enough coin to satisfy me, but you may try." She turned away, then spun back to face Bethia. "My dear, all he cares about is building ridiculous contraptions. Do not be foolish, although—" she glanced up and down Bethia's body, "—mayhap he's all you'll get."

Bethia whispered, "Your opinion means naught to me. Clearly, you think a woman's value is only in her looks. I have far greater assets, but you should stay out of the sun. Those wrinkles around your eyes will continue to grow deeper."

Glenna's eyes widened. She reached her hand back to slap Bethia, but Donnan stayed it. "Go, or I'll call the guard to drag you away. You have no say here. You denounced Clan Ramsay."

She picked up her skirts and spun on her heel, mumbling and cursing all the way out of the forest.

Donnan glanced at Bethia and took two steps forward until he stood close enough to kiss her. She didn't move, confusion and uncertainty in her gaze. He cupped her face and kissed her hard. She moaned and parted her lips, allowing him access, and their tongues dueled in a furious battle. He kissed a path down her neck and reached down until his hands touched her hips and then her bottom, tugging her close. He'd guessed she would feel his erection against her skirts, but what she did next couldn't have surprised him more. She angled herself so his hardness hit her at just the right spot.

Donnan growled and his mouth descended on hers again as he ravished her, slanting and tasting every part of her before his lips moved to the small bone at the base of her neck.

"Never, never doubt your beauty, Bethia. You are the most stunning creature I've ever had the pleasure of holding in my arms. Forgive me for what I've put you through."

Her eyes blazed with passion and pain, if it were possible to experience both at the same time. She brought her hand up and rested it on his chin, her thumb delicately touching his lower lip. "I'm sorry for what happened to your son, but I know with all my heart that you did not intentionally hurt him. Shame on your wife for making you believe such an awful thing."

"I love you, Bethia. You have the biggest heart of anyone I've ever known."

She sighed and her voice came out in a whisper. "I'm falling in love with you, Donnan. But I still do not know what to do about it."

He leaned his head forward until his forehead touched hers. "Your love empowers me. It tells me I've finally done something right in my life to earn something of such value. My thanks for believing in me." He stepped back and held his hand out to her. "Come. I'll walk you back, my beauty."

She placed her hand in his and he was humbled by her trust in him.

But his world had crumbled because, much to his chagrin, he was once again a married man.

Once they found their way out of the forest, they searched the area for Glenna, both of them pleased to see she and her guards had left.

Bethia smiled at Donnan, loving the feel of his hand wrapped around hers. She could forget everything when she was around this man—the taunts, the threats, everything.

Even Glenna.

He dropped her hand and said, "I think I need to return home. There are too many people about for me. I enjoy the quiet." He did a small bow, whistled for the dogs, winked at her, and left.

Bethia watched him leave. He leaned down to pet each dog before he headed back toward his land, picking his bow up where he'd dropped it and checking to be sure he still had his dagger. The last thing he did before he broke into a run was peek back at her over his shoulder and mouth the words, "I love you."

She nodded, placing her hand on her heart.

The sound of the races beckoned to her, for it had built up in volume, telling her they were drawing closer to the end. The last race was everyone's favorite—the deerhounds. If she didn't hurry back, Torrian would come looking for her. As she reached the edge of the crowd, surrounded by Ramsay guards, Bothan appeared at her side.

"Greetings, my lady." Bothan was an attractive enough man, but not as good-looking as Donnan.

She chastised herself for the direction her thoughts always turned. "Greetings, Bothan. Are you enjoying the races?"

"Aye. Torrian's dogs usually win, though there are some good contenders this year." His hand reached to the small of her back and he ushered her toward the bellowing crowd of enthusiastic supporters.

Henson appeared on her other side. "Greetings, Lady Bethia."

"Greetings, Henson."

He moved past her and said, "Why are you here, Bothan? The lady prefers my company, for certes. Take your leave, if you please."

Bothan's face turned as red as the Grant plaid they saw on occasion. "For certes, she prefers me. Is that not right, Lady Bethia?"

Bethia glanced from one to the other, shocked that Henson

would dare approach her after the way their walk had ended. His face still bore the mark of her fist. She wasn't quite sure how to handle it, but her gut told her that it didn't matter. These were two very immature lads, quite different from the tortured but kind man she'd just left.

Her mother rescued her. "Bethia, there you are. Lads, would you mind if I had a word with my dear daughter?"

Both of them turned to answer her mother, agreeing to her request and nodding to her before stepping away. The two of them continued to argue as they stepped away, their voices far louder than they likely thought they were.

"You're only interested in her because she's the laird's sister."

"Not true, but if it were, 'tis better than you wishing to be next to her if she's declared Queen of the Festival. If I recall, she was not pleased with your last encounter, Henson. Leave her be."

"I'm sure she prefers me, so please do not bother us again. I have plans for later."

"And I have plans for the two of us, as well. Stand back and let our romance begin. Do not get in my way, or I'll call a duel." After that, the sound of their bickering finally faded.

Bethia let out a huge sigh and stared at her mother. "What am I to do?"

"You are not interested in either one, are you?" her mother whispered. "Your heart belongs to another already. I can see it whenever he's near. Where did he go?"

"I cannot hide aught from you, Mama. Aye, 'tis true. I believe Donnan has my heart, but the situation does confuse me." She managed to pull her mother away from the crowd a bit so they could talk privately. "Mama, I met Glenna."

Her mother sighed loudly. "I heard she was here. What did she want?"

"She threatened him. She came back because she heard the old earl has passed. She wants Donnan to accept his inheritance, become Earl of Cairnie Castle. She wishes to be a countess."

"And how was Donnan with her?"

"He does not have any feelings for her, at least any warm feelings. That was quite clear, and his lack of love was reciprocated. She was not kind at all, only demanding."

"And did Donnan put an end to her demands?"

Her eyes misted at the memory of Donnan's posture and the expression on his face when his wife accused him of the worst crime possible.

"What is it? Tell me, child."

Her mother put her arms around her and all she could do was bury her face in her mother's shoulder. "She accused him of killing their son. He told me what happened, how the babe had been crying. Glenna ignored him, so Donnan picked him up from the cradle and took him to bed with him. He was dead by morn, and Glenna accused him of suffocating him."

"That is nonsense. It was then, and it is now. I was there. Bairns have been known to take their last breath for no reason. She cannot blame the babe's death on him with no proof."

Brenna pulled back to look at her mother. She whispered, "She threatened him, Mama. If he doesn't resume the marriage and accept the earldom, she'll tell our king that he murdered their son."

Her mother closed her eyes and sighed. "Bethia, she cannot do any such thing. As I said, she has no proof. I was there in the morn and I saw no evidence of such a thing. I could testify to our king. However…"

She didn't like her mother's last word. "What is it?"

"However, she does pose a definite problem."

"What?"

Her mother shook her head as if to deny everything that had transpired. "He's still married. If she accepts him as her husband now, I know not how he can arrange to end the marriage." She brushed the stray hairs back from her daughter's face.

"I was afraid you'd say that." She sniffled, doing the best to stop her tears before they flooded her cheeks. Why had she lost her heart to a married man?

"I'll talk to your sire and Uncle Logan. Mayhap they can see another way out of this for Donnan. Glenna was not a nice woman, and she *did* desert him."

"She has not changed a bit."

Shouts from the small platform that had been set up at the end of the field caught their attention. Uncle Logan waved everyone over. "Join me for the special announcement. Our Queen of the Festival will be chosen soon and given a crown of flowers to wear for the day."

Her mother grabbed her hand and tugged her in his direction.

"Mama, what is Uncle Logan about? Why is he doing this?"

"I know not, but we're about to see."

They reached the edge just in time for the announcement.

"So the verra first Ramsay Queen of the Festival has been chosen. She is the lass with the warmest heart of all and deserves our congratulations."

Someone tugged on her mother's sleeve. "My lady, someone has fainted. Could you check on her please? She's carrying and she passed out in the field."

"Of course," her mother said as the messenger hurried away.

"Mama, would you like my help?"

"Nay, 'tis a fainting. Quite common in those carrying late. Stay and listen to Uncle. I want to hear all about it," she whispered at the end. Then she took off after the messenger.

Bethia turned back to her uncle, still standing in front of the large crowd filled with many hopeful lasses.

"And the first Ramsay Queen is…"

Everyone leaned forward in anticipation of his announcement, and Uncle Logan did his best to drag it out.

"And the winner is…"

More leaning.

"Bethia Ramsay."

CHAPTER EIGHTEEN

B ETHIA'S KNEES BUCKLED AND SHE did her best not to
faint. She didn't want to give her mother another patient to
treat. In a state of shock, her feet didn't move until she was pushed
from behind amidst all the cheering. Somehow, she managed to
ascend the platform, and her uncle hugged her and placed the
crown of flowers on her head.

He whispered, "You deserve this. Do not listen to anyone who
says otherwise."

So that was why he'd done this.

She turned toward the crowd and forced a smile, staring down at
a sea of smiling faces and, aye, a few angry ones. Those lasses were
apparently upset that she had been chosen instead of them.

She wished to throw the crown into a loch and punch her uncle
for doing this to her.

Climbing down from the platform, she moved as if in a trance,
thanking all the well-wishers, ignoring the others. Lily, Maggie,
and Sorcha came up to hug her, Jennet and Brigid directly behind
them. Brigid jumped up and down, clapping her hands together
with excitement.

"I'm so happy, Bethia. You are the new queen. You deserve it."

Lily hugged her, and Bethia whispered, "Why would he do this
to me?"

Lily said, "I know not, but I'll talk to him."

Her family disappeared into the crowd, so she made her way
toward the great hall. Night was beginning to fall, and she wished
to get inside before the tears fell down her cheeks. The crowd
moved with her, as the end of the festivities usually included a

huge feast of food and ale for all. At least she could hide in her chamber, claim illness. She searched the area for her mother, but could not find her.

Gormal and Mor came boldly up to her. Mor said, "You do not deserve that crown. It belongs to Colina. She is the most beautiful of all."

"Aye, it should have been Colina's," Gormal added.

Bethia decided to ignore them. She kept moving toward the hall, following the path past the rows of cottages toward the gates and then into the courtyard. Many congratulations came her way, but she also heard other comments.

"It should have been Colina."

"She's too heavy."

"Why would they choose her?"

"She's the laird's sister, that's why."

She was almost to the steps of the hall when an arm grabbed her and yanked her around.

Colina.

"I knew it would go to you. You lied to me, said you never entered."

"I did not enter. Why do you care? I'll agree that you are beautiful, but this crown is meaningless."

Colina's hands went to her hips "If 'tis so meaningless to you, then why do you wear it?" A small crowd of onlookers had gathered around them.

Bethia closed her eyes and shook her head. "It means naught to me. If it means so much to you, you take it." She reached up and removed the crown, tossing it to the ground. "I do not want it."

She spun around and entered the hall, pushing her way toward the kitchens at the back of the hall. She'd rather run to her chamber, but pride stopped her.

Once she reached the back of the hall, she paused to gather herself and entered the kitchens, knowing all the serving lasses would be in the back, watching her every move. "Good eve to you, Cook. What have you on the night's menu?"

"Many wonderful meat pies. 'Twas a lovely day for the festivities, was it not?"

"Aye. Have you seen Mama?"

"Aye. She came in for some broth and took her leave to escort a lass to her hut. She was not feeling well and your mother didn't wish to leave her alone."

"My thanks. I think I'll assist her." She moved through the kitchens and headed out the back door. She needed to get away, and this was as good an excuse as any.

Rather than take the main path, she circled around to the gates, slipped through them, and glanced in the direction of their small village, trying to determine how to find her mother. There were many paths to the cottages, and it was now dark, though there were many torches that lit the path because of the festivals.

Cailean yelled to her, "She went that way, Bethia," pointing to the left.

Bethia thanked him and moved down the path he'd indicated, not seeing any evidence of her mother. More bellows and shouts were heard from behind her as those who'd already ingested too much ale began to leave the hall. Cailean and the other guards would have their hands full.

As she came to the end of the row of cottages, a voice called to her.

"She's over here."

Bethia moved in that direction, turned the corner, and stared straight at a fist heading directly toward her.

It was the last thing she remembered.

❧

Donnan was filling a bucket with water from the stream when he heard approaching horses. A small group of guards reined to a stop outside his hut. Quade Ramsay, on one of the lead mounts, shouted at him, "Donnan, have you seen Bethia?"

He turned to face the group, his gut clenching. "Nay. I have not seen her since the festivities. Why?"

"She's missing," Quade replied. "No one's seen her since she was given the title."

"The title?" Her father was clearly concerned, and he felt worry for Bethia wash over him. What had happened?

Logan Ramsay said, "I gave her the title of Queen of the Festival."

Donnan lost all ability to reason. "Why would you embarrass her like that?"

"Embarrass her?" Logan sounded genuinely baffled by the idea. "I gave her the reward she deserves for being the wonderful, caring, unselfish person she is. I'm tired of hearing others taunt her because of her size, which does not matter at all."

"And do you think the other lasses will view it that way?" Donnan was furious, barely squelching his desire to choke Logan Ramsay for his foolishness. "And what do you think those cruel lasses said to her about winning? Have you not heard them tease her? Why, 'twas why she ran away the night of her party. I'm sure she swallowed her pride and accepted your prestigious award, but an hour later, she probably ran away."

"Ran away?" Logan glanced at his brother, giving him an incredulous look.

"Clearly you know naught about your niece." He glared first at Logan and then at Quade to see how they accepted his declaration. How could they know so little about her? He knew. Because the lass he loved did nothing to draw attention to herself. She'd gone beneath their notice for too long, her sweetness blinding them to other aspects of her character—her doubts and questions, her passion and anger.

"And how would you know?" Logan asked.

Donnan dropped his voice to a whisper. "Because I love her. I know how the barbs from the other lasses her age affect her. You're either blind, or you're choosing to ignore it."

Logan emitted a low-sounding growl.

"Enough, Logan," Quade said. "He's correct. Brenna shared with me how Bethia feels. Donnan, assume we agree with you. Where do you think she could have gone?"

Logan dismounted and started pacing in a circle a good distance from Quade and Donnan. "You've searched your castle, I'm sure."

"Aye. Her mother is beside herself with worry because of Bearchun."

The sweat dripped out of Donnan's pores at the thought of Bethia in the hands of the addled man who'd hurt his dear Wynda. He went inside for a moment and brought something out.

Logan stopped his pacing abruptly. "What the hell is that?"

Donnan glared at him and replied, "This is one of the linen squares Bethia brought to use on Wynda. She dropped it." He didn't admit that he'd *seen* her drop it and purposefully kept it for himself. Her sweet scent was intoxicating. "My dogs will follow the scent."

"Should we start here or go back to the keep?" Quade asked.

"I say we go back to the keep to pick up the freshest scent. I've trained the hounds to spread out in search of it. We have no time to lose." He mounted his horse and whistled for the dogs to follow him. Before Logan had fully mounted, Donnan flicked the reins of his horse and headed back toward the Ramsay castle, the animals following him, even Wynda.

He pushed his horse, but the guards were still directly behind him. Once they reached the keep, he dismounted and whistled for the dogs. "Where was she last seen?"

Cailean, who'd fallen in with them, pointed to the end of one row of cottages in the village. "I sent her down this row after her mother, though Brenna never saw her."

Donnan knelt down at the end of the row and called the dogs to him. He held the linen square out to each of them in turn, allowing them to learn her scent. Torrian came down the row with a few of his own hounds.

"Hold on to that, Donnan. Here's another piece of her clothing," he said. "We'll set them all off at once and see what happens."

He did as his laird instructed, allowing the dogs to sniff the different pieces of cloth. He rubbed Wynda's ear and said, "I know you're a bit slower than usual, but you have the best nose. Find the right direction and we'll send the others ahead."

Wynda wagged her tail, took another sniff of the linen square, and then set off to do her job.

Torrian stood and said to the rest of the hounds, "Go. Find my sister." Then he waved the pack off. They followed his instructions and went off in different directions, their noses pressed to the ground.

Logan said to Torrian, "You do not truly think this will work, do you? I can track her better than the dogs."

"But in which direction, Uncle? The dogs can narrow it down and send us on the correct path. They'll pick her scent up in half an hour and they could save us several hours."

As if on cue, Wynda's tail wagged and she barked, calling Donnan to her. He ran over to her and a couple of other dogs picked up the same scent. Torrian said, "Mount up. Let them lead us as far as they can."

They headed off into the forest, the pack of dogs leading the charge.

They hadn't gone far when Logan jumped off his horse and into the bushes. He pulled a piece of fabric off a branch and stared at it. "Does this look like what she was wearing, Quade?"

His brother nodded.

The group continued on in the same manner for quite some time. They'd travel a bit, and Logan would find another piece of fabric, convincing them that they were on the right track.

Donnan felt sick to his stomach. They'd ridden far enough into the forest that he knew one thing for certain. Bethia hadn't just wandered off on her own—she'd been dragged away, kidnapped, stolen. Where in the hell was she?

The Ramsays were convinced Bearchun had kidnapped her, but he wasn't so sure. His wife had just left the area with two guards. She could have more hidden. Was she capable of such an evil act?

The further they traveled, the more clues turned up...and the more unsettled he became. This was too easy. What ultimately convinced him was Wynda's behavior. At one point, she became confused, running in circles and whining, very uncharacteristic of her.

That's when he knew what he had to do. "Ramsay!"

Logan and Quade both stopped their horses. "What is it?" Logan asked.

"We're going the wrong way."

"What?"

"I think we're going in the wrong direction. This is too easy. Wynda isn't acting right."

Logan glared at him. "I'm sorry, but I'll not change my actions based on a dog 'not acting right.' I've seen the evidence with my own eyes. We're staying on this track."

"Fine. I'll follow my instincts and head this way."

"Suits me. Go, Donnan."

He didn't wait. He called his dogs off and changed directions. There was no good reason for his sudden change, only instinct.

His gut told him the others were going the wrong way.

CHAPTER NINETEEN

LOGAN RAMSAY'S HEAD PAINED HIM from all the doubt and chaos. His dear niece was missing, and he feared she might have been kidnapped by Bearchun.

Donnan's announcement that he was going the wrong way had made him uneasy. He'd always been the best tracker in the clan, hadn't he? So how could he be wrong?

But something Donnan had said rang true. It was all too easy. Even so, he had to see it finished before he followed Donnan.

After he found the fifth scrap of clothing, they started to hear noises. Torrian turned toward the others and held his hand up to signal quiet. Sure enough, they heard voices in a clearing ahead, though they weren't close enough to make out any words.

Logan dismounted and crept up to the group, hiding behind bushes, Cailean behind him. One had his back to him. He listened, wanting to see what they knew about Bethia, if anything. The one facing him was definitely not Bearchun, but the one with his back to him could be.

He almost salivated with excitement at the prospect of finally getting his hands on the bastard who had tortured his family with pain and worries for months.

Both kept their voices low but laughed about something. He held his breath until he could make out their words.

"All those Ramsay bastards think they're smarter than everyone."

"They'll see the truth of it, will they not? We'll show them." The man chortled with glee.

Logan could stand it no longer. He burst into the clearing, cut the one facing him down with one swing of his sword, then threw his weapon down and jumped on the remaining one. "I'll kill you with my bare hands, Bearchun. You'll not live after touching my niece. Where is she?" He wrestled the lout to the ground on his back, pulled his fist back, and aimed it at the villain's face, only then realizing something shocking.

It wasn't Bearchun.

He stood up and grabbed the fool by the neck. "Where is my niece?"

Quade and Torrian burst in behind him, the guards surrounding them in an instant.

"I'll ask again before I choke the life out of you. Where is my niece?"

The man dared to smile at him. "You'll never find 'em."

"The hell I won't." Logan threw him against a tree and started to pummel him. Every two punches, he paused to ask him, "Where? Where is she?"

Torrian moved over and stilled his hand. "Did he say them?"

Logan must have heard wrong. "What the hell are you talking about?"

"He said, 'find 'em.' Who is them?"

The man guffawed, throwing his head back. "Bearchun was right. He knew we could pull you off the real trail. You'll never find them. You followed the wrong trail, and now they're way ahead of you. 'Twas brilliant to tear her clothing and leave pieces for you and the dogs. Now you'll never find them without my help."

Logan called two guards over and said, "Hold him."

Quade yelled at him. "You need to keep him alive, Logan. He's the only one we have. You killed the other."

"I'll keep the bastard alive." He punched him in the belly twice, then said, "Where are they?"

The man coughed but said naught.

Logan dragged him over to the bushes off to the side. "Do you see those nettles? I'm going to lay your bollocks in them and drag you across them until you scream your answer."

The prisoner's eyes widened, but he said naught. Logan couldn't wait any longer. He said to the guards, "Remove his plaid. You'll each take one leg, and we'll force him down on the nettles, bollocks first."

The man attempted to cover his bollocks, but Logan kneed

him first. The man doubled over in pain and said, "I'll tell, I'll tell. Please, no more."

"Where are they?"

The man heaved once and said, "He split them up. She has Bethia and he has the wee ones."

Logan closed his eyes, unable to believe this had happened to them again.

"Where?"

"Cairnie Castle."

"Tie him to the tree and take his weapons," Logan said. "If he's lying, we'll be back."

Logan strode over to his horse.

Torrian and Cailean were quick behind him. "What's your plan?" Torrian asked.

"Go back and get more warriors. We're headed to Cairnie Castle."

Quade limped behind his brother. "You have a sick look on your face I don't like. He must have Jennet and Brigid. The guards will already be searching for them. Mayhap they've found them. Why the look?"

"And Donnan knew we were going the wrong way," Torrian said. "Mayhap he's already saved Bethia. We could be in luck."

Logan stopped before he mounted his horse, waiting for his brother to catch up. "You could all be correct. Mayhap this has ended already, but one fact is niggling at me."

"What?"

"Who do you think the woman at Cairnie Castle is?"

"Glenna," Cailean said immediately. "Donnan's wife was here earlier. Must have been a trick."

"Hell, mayhap Sorcha did choose well." He clasped his son-in-law's shoulder. "Cailean's right," he said as he peered at his brother and his nephew.

"Glenna must be part of this, and she is daft. Our lasses will be split up, which makes the situation so much worse."

They mounted up in silence, the truth weighing them down.

"I pray Donnan has been able to find Glenna and Bethia," Logan finally said. "At least he had traveled ahead of us."

⟨⟩

Bearchun picked at the remainder of the scab across his face. He forced himself to stare at the bloody bit of scab, doing his best to convince himself he was cured of his strange affliction. Hellfire, but the thing still itched terribly. Then he rubbed the wound on his shoulder. That bastard had caught him good, though it wasn't his sword arm. When would his agony end?

He smiled. It was about to end. All he had to do was tolerate the foolish bitch who continued to annoy him.

"You promised me if I helped you that you'd bring me to Cairnie Castle and I could be the princess of the castle." She flung her red hair back over her shoulder.

He glared at her, stopping as he paced in front of the small cottage where he'd taken the lasses. "Did you truly believe me? Because there is no such thing as a princess in the land of the Scots—only Margaret, and your name is not Margaret. You would have to go to London, then see if you could find yourself a prince to marry. 'Tis the only way you can be a princess, though you can keep wearing that foolish crown on your head all you please."

"I'm Queen of the Festival. I need to go back." Her hands went to her hips and she glared at him. "I just wished to help you tie up Bethia. I hate her. But I don't hate the wee ones. Why did you have to steal them away?"

She spun on her heel and strode away from him. "I'm leaving. You lied to me. You told me I could be a princess."

"I wouldn't go back that way on your own, lass."

"Why not? I can find my way. Gormal is probably looking for me." She continued on her way, ignoring him.

"Because there is a steep ravine up ahead and you may not see well enough in the dark. If you are not careful, you may hurt yourself. Go to the left a bit."

The foolish chit listened to him and moved to the left, exactly where the ravine was located. A few seconds later, he heard a scream and then a sound of crunching bones that made him laugh. He waited until she landed at the bottom with a thud. Deciding to go after her, he trudged toward the ravine, though chances were good that she'd run into a boar or a couple of snakes at the bottom.

Dead silence.

He peered over the edge of the ravine. "Colina?"

No answer. He crawled down a few rocks, looking for her. She was a pretty lass, though her attitude was difficult at best. When he found her, he turned away and said, "Ouch." The tumble over the edge had snapped her neck. She lay dead in a heap.

He shook his head and climbed back up the side, being careful not to end up in the same condition. He trudged back to the cottage, scratching his scar again. "Foolish twit."

Once inside the cottage, he lit a torch. The bigger of the two lassies was awake.

She sat up and stared at him. "I curse you," she whispered.

He chuckled. "You can't do much all tied up the way you are. Curse me all you want, but even I know a witch needs her hands to cast her spells."

Jennet said, "Aye, I can still curse you. I send spiders down to lay their eggs in your fresh scar. You know they like new skin, do you not?"

A spider landed on his shoulder and he screamed loud enough to awaken the other one, Brigid. He shoved the creature off him and stepped on it. "I know, you only said that because you saw it coming toward me. I'm not a fool."

She cackled and Brigid stared at him wide-eyed. "What are you going to do with us?" the wee lassie asked with a whimper.

"I'm waiting for your sire to come for you. I want Logan and Torrian Ramsay to pay. I would say Quade, too, but he's feeble now. But not to worry, they'll be here soon." He spun on his heel and laughed on his way back out the door.

He'd kill Logan Ramsay. But not before the man realized that Bearchun had killed his daughter and two of his beloved nieces. He would be glad to end Jennet's life. A small part of him knew it was wrong. She was just a wee lassie, but she'd cursed him again. He didn't like witches.

Revenge would finally be his, and it would be sweet, total, and devastating to the Ramsays.

CHAPTER TWENTY

ʃ

DONNAN ARRIVED AT CAIRNIE CASTLE in the middle of the night. The castle appeared deserted. He wondered where his sister and her husband could be.

He did love his sister. He'd loved his sire until he'd abandoned him, unwilling to accept Glenna. It still stung that his sire had been right. He'd seen Glenna's black soul from the beginning.

His heart threatened to choke him because he had no idea if he'd been wrong to follow his gut, but something had told him Glenna was involved in Bethia's kidnapping. He had another bad feeling about the silence in the castle, as if no one was here. He wished he'd brought his dogs with him, but after realizing how long the journey would be, he'd sent them home out of worry for Wynda.

A sound carried through the night. Cairnie Castle did not have a large village the way Ramsay Castle did. There were three cottages behind the castle for the servants, and one on the opposite side for the steward of the property.

He crept around the outside of the castle and heard sounds inside the closest cottage, the one for the steward. It was a woman's voice.

Glenna.

He didn't wait. He burst into the cottage and took her by surprise. However, she didn't look disappointed—a sick smile stretched across her face at the sight of him. He scanned the cottage for any sign of Bethia, but she didn't appear to be there. There was a table and chairs, one pallet on the floor and two trunks on either side. A hearth waited at the farthest end of the chamber.

"Donnan, I've been expecting you."

"Where's Bethia?"

"She is well hidden. As soon as I gain your agreement, I'll tell you where to find her." She sat down at the table and drummed her fingers on the top. "Well? What is your answer?"

"Agreement to what?" he ground out.

"I've already told you, and I think you should know by now that I don't give up. I don't just want money from you, you see, I wish to be a countess. *A countess.* The same thing I've always wanted. With coin and jewels at my fingertips." She held her hand up in the air, wiggling her fingers for drama. "Why is that so hard, Donnan? You accept your inheritance, we move into Cairnie Castle, you give me unlimited access to your funds, and I become the Countess of Cairnie Castle."

"It is difficult because I do not want that life. And because I love Bethia. She has a bigger heart than anyone I know…"

"And a bigger arse…"

He stormed across the cottage, giving her no opportunity to finish her sentence. "Do not disparage her. She is as beautiful as any lass I've ever known, and even more beautiful on the inside than she is on the outside."

"Go ahead. Choke me. Kill me as you did our son."

Donnan stepped back, but he refused to sit, choosing instead to pace. His nervousness about Bethia—was she hale? Had Glenna hurt her?—had steadily grown on his journey to the castle. Now it was even keener, because he'd realized his worst fear was true.

Glenna was daft.

☾

Bethia listened from inside the crate where she was imprisoned, struggling against her bindings and the horrid-tasting gag in her mouth. If she could just manage to make some noise, Donnan would know she was here.

Then the words she heard made her freeze.

Donnan loved her.

True, he'd told her so before, but a part of her had wondered if he was being truthful. The other lads who'd pursued her seemed to have ulterior motives for doing so. Bothan, mayhap because she was Torrian's sister and Quade's daughter, and Henson had his mind on her breasts. Some fear had told her that mayhap Donnan, sweet, handsome Donnan, had his own secret reasons for pursuing her. Now she knew his love was true. She blinked back the tears that threatened to drench her cheeks, not wanting to cry in such close surroundings.

She listened to more.

"Glenna, why would you choose to live with me again?"

"Why not? We got along fine until we ran out of coin." Bethia could just imagine Glenna's terrible beauty, her eyes alight with madness. "Do you not think my hands should be covered with jewels? Rubies…rubies were always my favorite."

Donnan had to make her see reason. He had to calm her down enough for them to escape this situation with their lives. "We never got along once we lost Donnie. I couldn't live with the guilt. There are many times I have considered taking my own life."

Bethia gasped at this admission. How his heart must have ached after losing his son. He was not the type to commit such an act unless driven by a grief so powerful, so consuming that he believed it was his only escape.

How terrible for anyone to feel such pain.

Glenna's cold voice interrupted her thoughts. "Please do the deed *after* you claim your inheritance. Then the castle will be mine as your widow."

"Nay, 'twill be my sister's. I have written a will denouncing you and leaving the property to my sister."

Bethia did not hear any response to Donnan's revelation. Glenna had to be carefully considering her next words. She heard the shuffling of feet.

"Och, Donnan. Please do not take your own life. I would feel responsible."

Silence again. Glenna had to be attempting to use her wiles on Donnan.

Donnan huffed. "I do not believe you. Why would you suddenly take on any responsibility? 'Tis not your way."

She heard footsteps move away from her, then back toward her, then away from her again.

"Why do you pace? What is it you're not telling me, Glenna? I know you wish me to be unburdened of any connection to me—beyond my inheritance—but why hurt Bethia? Could you live with the guilt of two deaths on your conscience?"

Glenna's voice came out as a shriek and Bethia could almost see the sick fury in her eyes. "For heaven's sake, Donnan. Stop with your self-righteous behavior. I cannot kill you—and you cannot kill yourself—until you change the will."

"And why should I do that?"

"Because I wish to be the countess."

"Nay, I'll not do that. My sister deserves to be in the castle. She and her husband have taken good care of it. Where are they?"

"They were sent away. Change your will."

Silence hung in the cottage for a moment before he said, "Free Bethia and I'll agree. You can have whatever you want as long as you promise not to hurt her."

"Fine, I'll free her, but you must promise to change the will... and you cannot leave me. You must stay by my side. To prove I have a generous heart, I'll even allow you to bring Bethia with you. You may sleep in her bed every night as long as you give me what I want."

"Free Bethia and I'll move into the foolish castle with you. I'll accept you as my wife in name, but I'll not subject her to *you*. I'd prefer to see her happy."

His voice grew louder and louder, and her heart ached at the pain he was going through. At the sacrifices he was willing to make for her.

"But know this. Every day we live together, I'll be reminded of my guilt in causing Donnie's death. Seeing you will remind me. Do you know how many days that thought has been the first in my mind when I awaken? Every day, the first thing that I think of is Donnie. A son. I had a son." He paused. "Free Bethia, and I'll live with you, but do not expect us to get along. Or for me to bear the pain forever. But I'll do my best to make sure you have enough coin first, you shallow bitch."

"Fine, fine. I'll admit it. You never killed Donnie. *I* did. I was sick of his screaming and crying and dirty raggies, and I'd had enough. I never wanted him. Never wanted to be tied to you. I just wanted the title and your money."

Bethia stopped breathing. Had she heard Glenna correctly? Was she capable of such a fiendish act? Killing her own bairn? But if she spoke the truth, it also meant that Donnan had not done it. She'd killed her own flesh and blood and allowed another to bear the burden of it.

Donnan's voice came out in a whisper. "What did you do, Glenna?"

Glenna continued to shout. "I killed the screaming brat. When you fell asleep, he started to cry again, so I took the coverlet and covered his nose and mouth. I did it. I could not tolerate listening to him anymore."

"You killed him? You killed our son and made me believe I did it? All these years I've suffered the burden of guilt for no reason?"

Bethia heard the movement of feet, indicating he was moving toward Glenna.

"I would wake up from nightmares of Donnie staring at me with his eyes open, unable to breathe. Do you know how many nights I had that same dream? Do you? You cold-hearted bitch."

Silence.

"I'd like to choke all the air out of you the way you did my son. Where. Is. Bethia?" Donnan's tone made her shiver.

Silence reigned again.

A loud banging followed, Bethia guessed he'd slammed his fists on a piece of furniture, or mayhap the wall.

Bethia thought she would vomit. How she wished to wrap her arms around Donnan to help him through this horror. No matter what, she had to stop him from hurting Glenna. Donnan's gentle soul would never be able to live with such an act, despite all the woman had done to ruin him.

Bethia rocked her body in the crate, sobbing and crying for the man she loved, knowing she would do anything for him.

"What the hell? That trunk is moving."

"Stay back, Donnan. You have to agree. You promised me."

"I promised you nothing unless you freed Bethia, and you have not."

She heard the sound of someone shrieking, then a slight thud— as if a slender body had fallen a slight distance—and then the top of the trunk finally opened. Ah, Glenna had tried to shield the trunk with her body, and Donnan had not allowed it.

Bethia squinted at the light from the candles, still crying from what she'd just learned. Donnan smiled at the sight of her, but it did naught to banish the pain from his eyes. The door opened, and they both turned to watch Glenna leave.

After he yanked the cloth out of her mouth, he reached in to cup her cheek. "Bethia? You are hale?"

She nodded, unable to make her jaw work enough to speak. He helped her sit up, then lifted her out of her prison as though she weighed nothing more than a feather in the breeze. He sat in the nearest chair and settled her on his lap, fumbling with the ties that bound her hands and feet.

When she finally could speak, she whispered, "Donnan, your son. I'm so sorry."

He cupped her face and kissed her lips, then kissed each tear that had managed to slide down her cheek. "Hush. Please do not speak of it yet. I'm numb. But know that I love you and I must get you out of here safely."

She could see the tears on his face. Had she ever seen a man cry so openly? "I love you. I'll help you through this." She gripped his shoulders, wanting to do something to ease his pain, but she also recognized the peril they were in had not yet abated. "Where do you think she went?"

He swiped at his tears and helped her to her feet. "Can you stand? I'm sure your legs are tight from the confinement."

She managed to bear her weight, clutching his arm as if she never wanted to let him go.

The door burst open, and three unknown guards stood blocking the door, two with daggers and the other with a sword. "Bearchun wants you both."

CHAPTER TWENTY-ONE

◠

B EARCHUN RUBBED HIS SCAR AGAIN.
Today was the day he'd finish it. He'd make them all appreciate him, regret their taunting. He'd show them all who was the
strongest, the mightiest of all the warriors. Wee Jennet had the
power to bring back his aversion to blood, but she was tied up,
unable to work her magic. He wouldn't faint this eve. He was sure
of it.

He stepped out of the cottage and gathered his soldiers.

"Here is the plan. I want Logan Ramsay. We have his daughter
and two of his nieces. I will bring him to his knees before I kill
him. I'm leaving two of you here to guard the lassies. Do not
move until I call you out to the front of the gates." He pointed to
the grouping on the other side of the castle. "The beauty of this
set-up is they will not be able to see you, but you'll be able to hear
everything we say.

A man armed with a bow and arrow stood in front of him.
"Where do you want me?" Earc asked. "Let me kill one of them,
please? I want them so bad I can taste it."

Earc had been one of Ranulf's associates, and he, too, had a bitter taste in his mouth about the Ramsays. They'd ended Ranulf's
quest for riches—which meant his followers had found themselves
poverty stricken.

Bearchun grasped his shoulder and said, "Relax. You'll have the
pleasure of taking Logan's niece out. The big one."

Earc smiled, pleased with his assignment.

"When Logan arrives, I'm going to challenge him to a fist fight.
I can't beat the man with a sword, and I don't dare choose a bow,

but he's old. I can easily take him with my fists. I want to see his face up close as he watches his loved ones die. So I'm going to fight him for a few punches, then Earc—" he pointed to the smiling fool, "—you're going to put an arrow in Bethia's heart. When he sees that happen, he'll be so upset that he won't be able to fight, and I'll easily beat him to the ground.

"Once I have him down, I'll whistle for you two to bring the wee lassies over, and I'll torture his daughter in front of him. Whoever does the best job gets to kill the witch after we've finished him."

"What about the rest of the Ramsay guards? They'll kill you before any of that happens."

"If they don't know where the two wee ones are, they'll not touch me. I'll make sure the lassies are well hidden before I show my face. And when Logan and the Ramsay brats are all dead, Glenna says she'll get Donnan to fall into line. She'll let us into Cairnie Castle, and we'll lock the gates and use it as a fortress. Then her work is done and we agree to keep her involvement secret. As for the Ramsays, they'll be too stunned to stop us. Earc will be up in the trees, picking off any Ramsay guards who dare approach us. Once Bethia is dead, you can kill as many as you want, Earc."

Earc asked, "How will I know when you want me to kill Bethia?"

"I'll run my hand through my hair like this." He demonstrated the movement to Earc. "That's the signal to put an arrow through her heart."

Glenna came flying toward them, her movements frantic. "He found her," she shouted. "Kill her. You have to kill her, or I'll not get Donnan to comply." She stopped directly in front of him to make this statement.

Bearchun said, "Calm down. I have everything planned. But 'tis not yet time."

"Do it now. I told you when we met that you'd not push my wishes aside. I've given you everything you needed: information on how to kidnap the Ramsays, a place to hide after you've killed them, even four more men. You couldn't have done this without me. I expect you to do as you promised me in Edinburgh."

"Aye, I will. I'll kill Donnan and you can be countess."

"Nay, the agreement was you'd follow my instructions and act as my enforcer. Now I want you to keep him alive and kill *her*. He changed his will, so he's of no use to me dead. You have to help me."

He nodded. "Aye, but we do it my way. Understood?"

"Agreed. Now how do I protect myself?"

"Here—" he handed her a dagger, "—keep this with you in case something happens. Are you sure we can get inside the castle after all is over?"

"Aye, if the gates are locked, I know where the tunnel is. Everything else is already locked to outsiders."

"Where is Donnan's sister?"

"She and her husband traveled to Edinburgh to plead with the king, taking many of the servants with them. She hopes to find Donnan there, also. Once they left, my guards sent the rest away."

A guard raced over to them on his horse. "Ramsay plaids have been sighted."

"Can you tell which ones?" Bearchun asked.

"Aye. Logan and the laird are in the lead."

Bearchun smiled. "Perfect. Go to your spots and be ready."

"What about me?" Glenna asked.

"You hide in the bushes. I'll send guards over to bring Bethia to us. What about Donnan?"

Glenna snorted. "He's a mess. He'll go along with Bethia. But you must keep him alive."

Bearchun said, "Good. Our time is here. Go to your assignments."

☾

Bethia held onto Donnan with a death grip while he tried his best to reason with their captors. How she wished he hadn't caught the injury to his side. Uninjured, he could have taken all three guards, but she could feel the weakness in his body creeping up on him.

"I'll go to Bearchun willingly if you'll set the lady free. I'll give Glenna whatever she wishes. 'Tis no place for a lady in the middle of the night."

"Shut your mouth and keep moving. Bearchun wants the both of you, he does. You'll do exactly as he says."

They moved to the front of the castle, outside the open gates. Bethia could feel her legs giving out, but Donnan braced her against him. It was a comfort that he was with her, though now that they were in front of the castle, several other guards milled about, all armed.

She didn't see Glenna, but it wasn't long before her gaze found Bearchun's. A shiver ran all the way through her body.

He smiled and headed straight for them. As soon as he was close, Donnan said, "Let her go. I'll stay in her place. I'm the new Earl of Panmure. I'll give you and Glenna whatever coin you want. Just let her go."

Bearchun chortled. His finger ran down the side of Bethia's face, and Donnan shoved it away. "If 'tis not the gracious Bethia Ramsay, daughter of the old laird, sister to the new one. The verra Ramsay who allowed me to steal her sister and cousin away without a word. Although I must admit, you are one of the nicer ones, even if you are too large for my taste."

Bethia did her best to ignore his taunts. "What do you want?"

"Och, you are a bit bolder than you were before, aye? You'll see what I want. 'Tis quite simple. I wish to bring your uncle to his knees. He's the one who ruined my hopes of becoming a great warrior. He's the one who allowed your sister to play the witch, casting a spell over me."

"You'll never bring Uncle Logan to his knees. He's the best swordsman on our land, and his wife is the best archer. With all the other Ramsay guards, you'll not stand a chance against him." She lifted her chin a notch.

"Except for one small thing you seem to have forgotten. Or mayhap you do not know…aye, you probably do not." He stared off into the treetops of the mighty oaks nearby and tapped his finger on his chin. "I not only hold you, but I also have wee… hmmm…let me think for a moment." He tapped his chin and stared up at the cloudy night sky. "Aye, now I recall their names. Jennet and Brigid? Is that not correct?"

Bethia could not contain her gasp. Donnan squeezed her middle in a silent message of support.

Bearchun guffawed as he walked away. "Now you understand. I have all three of you. I will win this battle, and none of my men will lose a drop of blood." He winked at her as he paced in the opposite direction. "The lassies are well hidden, and your uncle will need me alive to find them. He will not dare have his bitch of a wife put an arrow in me. I have made sure to secure my safety."

She waited until he was gone to give into her fears. "Donnan," she whispered, "oh my, I cannot imagine my sister and Brigid..."

"Hush," he whispered back in her ear. "Do not yield to him. You must stay strong. We will win. Your brother, your uncle, Cailean. All mighty warriors. Have faith."

"No talking," one man behind them barked. "Bearchun, where do you want them?"

Bearchun walked around the area in front of the gates, meandering slowly as though he were planning something. He peered into the trees, glanced at distances and angles, then finally answered. "Move them twenty paces from that tree. And you'll stand side by side." The last place he glanced at was a small knoll to the right of the group.

What in hell was he planning? The guards moved them exactly where he'd instructed. Once they were in position, Bearchun's men moved back, hidden from view by the trees.

Donnan waited until they were out of range, then whispered, "Listen."

Bethia turned her head to the side and squeezed his hand as soon as she heard the thunder of horses' hooves in the distance.

Many, many horses.

She closed her eyes and said a prayer that it was the Ramsay warriors, her sister and cousin would survive, and all would be well. Where was her mother? What must she be going through?

Not ten minutes later, a cavalry of horses crested the small ridge in the distance and rumbled across the meadow, finally coming to a stop in front of them. Bethia's gaze searched the group, noting all the warriors she knew so well. Logan was in front with Torrian, Kyle by her brother's side. Cailean sat atop his destrier on Logan's other side, his brother, Alan, behind him. Her eyes shot to the rest of the row behind them, her heart in her throat.

Gavin, Gregor, Tormod, and even Henson and Bothan. She did not see her sire, thankfully, but she guessed he was not far. Her uncle Micheil and his son David sat a couple of rows back. How had they known? Aunt Avelina, the seer, must have had a vision and sent word. Uncle Micheil often appeared when they needed him most.

Bearchun's voice rang out as soon as they stopped, though he was not in clear view. "Shoot anyone now, Ramsay, and not only will Bethia die in front of you, but your daughter and your niece will, too. The wee lassies are well hidden, and you'll not find them if I'm dead."

"What do you want, Bearchun?" Uncle Logan's voice rang out loud and clear for all to hear, a voice known to strike fear in the Ramsays' enemies, and now she understood why. Her respect for the warriors of her clan grew by leaps and bounds as she observed them.

Bearchun's voice brought her back to the circumstances in front of her. "You, Logan Ramsay. I want you. Send your guards away, out of my sight, and you stay. Hand-to-hand combat, just you and me, with none of your warriors to back you up."

"And you promise not to shoot me down? Because naught would give me more pleasure than to snap your neck in my hands, Bearchun."

"You have my word as a former Ramsay warrior. No one will touch you or shoot at you but me. Send your men back."

"And when will you show yourself? Pardon me for not taking your word. You left the Ramsays long ago."

Uncle Logan acted as though he did this every day. Bethia's hands trembled, but her uncle looked as calm as could be.

Bearchun shouted, "Get rid of them and I'll show myself. And I wouldn't have anyone attempt to shoot the men guarding your niece. I have archers on her, ready to kill if you go near her."

Logan didn't speak, his gaze slowly traveling the area. "Bethia, you are hale?"

"Aye, Uncle." Her voice came out in a squeak as she gave the answer, her legs quaking underneath her.

His hand moved into his hair and then to his back before he turned his head and nodded to Torrian. "Take your leave."

"Are you sure, Uncle?"

"Aye. Please do not try to deny me this pleasure," Logan's voice came out in a deep growl that frightened even Bethia. "The bastard is mine, and I've been waiting a long time for this."

Bearchun guffawed.

"We will not be far." Torrian gave his signal and the horses all turned to the side at once, stirring up a bit of dirt as they rode away.

"Where exactly would you like me to kill you, Bearchun?"

CHAPTER TWENTY-TWO

ᕫ

LOGAN RAMSAY COULDN'T BE MORE pleased. The bastard wished to fight him in hand-to-hand combat. He'd beat the wastrel silly. He'd waited months for this opportunity—dreamed of it.

He wiped the sweat that dotted his forehead on his sleeve before he dismounted, standing next to his horse. He wouldn't step from his mount until Bearchun showed his face. He thought he saw a glimpse of him behind a set of bushes to his right, but he couldn't be sure in the dark.

The only thing that worried him was Bethia. His beautiful niece stood out in the open. Based on her position and how Donnan stood to her side, he had no doubt Bearchun had an archer on the wall with an arrow aimed at her heart. He'd known Donnan long enough to know the man would never allow a lass to stand unprotected unless he'd been ordered to do so.

He counted five men clearly visible, but he doubted the fool could have more than ten other men. He didn't have the following or the reputation of MacNiven, which had drawn fools to him like flies to sweet tarts.

Idiot. He'd make him pay dearly for all the aggravation he'd caused his family.

Bearchun thought he could take Logan Ramsay on in hand-to-hand...rather, fist-to-fist...combat? Ha! As soon as the bastard showed his face, he'd be all over him and prove him wrong.

There was only one problem—he'd have to keep his eye on Bethia at all times. He'd like to trust Donnan to protect her, but he could easily be outnumbered, especially since he'd been injured not long ago. Protecting her was on Logan's shoulders.

"I'm not stepping away from my horse until the slime comes out from under his rock." He'd play with Bearchun's head as much as he could. The lout had been in the Ramsay lists and he'd sparred with him, so he knew his weaknesses. Including the way he responded to barbs.

The arsehole didn't stand a chance.

He waited, listening to the hoot of an owl in the distance, training his vision to stay near Bethia. The smell of body odor wafting over him, the kind that came from being frightened and unable to calm the fear roiling inside in your gut—and it wasn't his.

His horse nickered, his warning to his master that someone had stepped out of the dark.

His gaze crossed the entire length of the curtain wall, trees running down both sides of the entrance.

Finally, he found him.

Bearchun stepped out from behind a tree and moved toward him, his hand reaching up to rub the fresh scar on his face. Donnan had described it well.

"We almost got you at Buchan Castle, aye?" Logan would taunt him as much as he could to unsettle him before he threw his first punch. "Was that my sword that found you?" He stepped in front of his horse, who pawed the ground as if to say he wanted a piece of the swine, too.

A smile crossed Logan's face, he just couldn't prevent it. He'd waited so long for this moment. Bearchun came a few paces closer before he halted, a man's length away from Logan but directly in front of the open gates to the castle.

The bastard meant to do something twisted because he'd left himself room to run—and a place to escape to.

Logan Ramsay would bring him down.

"I'm ready whenever you are, you piece of shit," he whispered to Bearchun. "Do your best before I flatten you." He flexed his fists to ready himself for battle, then spit to the side, checking Bethia with the slight tip of his head. She was frightened, but he caught a touch of strength in her, something new for his dear niece.

Bearchun came running straight at him with a growl. Logan pulled his fist back and hit him straight in his belly and, in the same movement, shifted and stuck his foot out to trip him, sending him face first into the ground.

Logan landed on Bearchun's back, his knee pinning him down while his hand yanked on his hair. "That didn't take long now, did it, big man? Do you want to take me on again?" He released him and Bearchun jumped to his feet, his fist swinging and then connecting with Logan's jaw, taking him by surprise.

"How'd that feel, Ramsay?" he cackled.

Logan spun around and kicked his leg out, catching Bearchun in the side of his head, knocking him to the ground. "Not as bad as that did, I'm quite sure."

Bearchun lost his temper, getting back to his feet and running low at Logan, hoping to lift him off his feet, but he couldn't move him. He'd misjudged his size and strength. Logan grabbed his leg and flipped him onto his back, knocking the wind out of him.

Logan leaped onto him, pummeling him everywhere he could. Bearchun began to kick and scream like a lass, much to his delight, so he gave him the chance to get to his feet. He wasn't ready to end it for him yet.

"That's the last time I'll allow you to get back up. Where's my daughter?"

Bearchun laughed, wiping the blood that poured down one side of his face. "You'll never find her. No one knows where she is but me. I dug a fresh hole for the two lasses. There is a crate buried underneath the earth with naught but a pipe sticking out of the ground. No one will ever see it. You should have heard them cry when I started to throw dirt on top of the crate."

Logan did something he never did. He lost all sense of reason. He lunged at the man, pushing at him until his back was up against a tree, and then he punched his gut, his face, aught he could bloody his knuckles on. "Where is she? Where is she?" His fists battered one side of the man's face, then the other.

Bearchun's hand reached up and ran through his hair. Logan was too slow to react, not recognizing it for the signal it was until he was too late.

Chaos ensued.

He turned toward Bethia at the same time he heard the arrow come from over his shoulder and slice through the air not far from his head, aimed straight for his beloved niece.

Everything slowed as he watched the arrow head straight for his dear niece's heart. The worst of it was that she had no idea. He screamed, "Down," but the shock on her face slowed her reaction. Her only response was to turn and look at him.

Bethia was a dead woman.

CHAPTER TWENTY-THREE

ɔ

D ONNAN SAW MOVEMENT IN ONE of the trees and turned
in that direction, only to see an arrow headed straight for his
love. He did the only thing possible—he stepped in front of Bethia
to protect her and turned his body just enough to catch the arrow
in his shoulder.

He threw her to the ground and covered her with his body,
afraid another arrow would soon follow. He glanced up at the
fools around them, who'd been caught off guard. Screams filled
the air, but he knew not who was screaming.

Bethia shouted his name and pushed against him. The pain that
rippled through his upper body was nothing compared to other
pain he'd experienced, both in battle and after Donnie's death, so
he held her down and said, "Hush, I'm fine, I'm fine. 'Tis only my
shoulder."

"You're hurt. Donnan. Get off me, please. They'll kill you." Her
fists banged against him with little strength, but he did not move
an inch. He had to protect her.

When several moments passed without another assault from
above, Donnan rolled off Bethia to determine the source of the
continued screaming. The guards who'd stood behind them had
slid over toward Bearchun, an expression of fear on their faces,
though he couldn't understand why. He and Bethia were unarmed.

Bethia sat up, looking about wildly. "What's happening? Where
is Uncle Logan?"

The scene before them was one of chaos. Men ran in different
directions, following the strange screaming, which seemed to be
getting closer to them. Beneath the sound, he could hear what

appeared to be the cries of animal. Logan had Bearchun by the throat, but they both froze and turned toward the uncanny, deafening clamor.

Donnan stood, pushing Bethia away from him in an attempt to protect her from whatever was headed toward them.

Out of the dark rushed a figure he recognized, coming straight for him, dagger raised over her head.

Glenna. The crazed screams had been from her.

Donnan braced himself for her attack, but to his amazement, she changed directions at the last minute and launched herself at Bethia, her teeth bared in a scream that carried across the area. "You bitch! You've ruined everything. I'll kill you!"

Donnan dove to protect Bethia, but his foot got caught on a rock and he lost his balance, falling to the ground, snapping the arrow out of his shoulder. He was powerless as Glenna leaped straight for Bethia, who backed up until she reached the curtain wall.

There was nowhere else for her to go, and he feared he would have to watch as his love was killed in front of him.

The most beautiful sight he'd ever seen came out of nowhere.

Shewolf charged straight at Glenna, her magnificent jaws latching onto the forearm of the hand that clutched the knife, the force of the beast's powerful body knocking her down at once. The animal pulled her away from Bethia and tossed her body up against a tree with a growl. The blow seemed to have killed Glenna instantly.

Bethia jerked her head away and ran straight for Donnan. He opened his arms for her and she fell into them, doing her best not to hurt his shoulder. The arrow was no longer visible, though a piece was surely still embedded inside. She would see to it later.

He hugged her, holding her tight, but then checked the area because chaos still reigned. Shewolf still roamed the area but none of Bearchun's guards would go near her.

Logan Ramsay had renewed his pummeling of Bearchun, whom he now had by the throat against a tree. "You'll take me to them now, or I'll snap your neck with my hands."

The wolf now stood a short distance from Logan, as if guarding his back, pacing back and forth.

"Hellfire, snap my neck because I'm not telling. I'll *never* tell." Bearchun's voice was weakening.

"I'll kill every one of your men in front of you until you tell me where they are." Two more punches to Bearchun's belly forced him to cough, but after three more gags, his coughing turned into evil laughter.

"I care not about any of them. Kill them all if you like. I'll still not tell." His laughter continued, but his comments had apparently registered with his men—they exchanged glances as if considering their next move.

A voice penetrated the night air, stronger and surer than the eerie laughter of the daft man. "Logan, stand back."

Bethia turned her head toward the voice just as Logan shifted his body, though he kept his hand on Bearchun's throat, still holding him against the tree.

An arrow flew out of the trees, aimed into the tree opposite where Donnan and Bethia were huddled. An archer came tumbling out of the tree at the same time a second arrow landed in Bearchun's flesh, pinning him to the tree.

Logan laughed and said, "Nice shot, Gwynie."

"Get out of the way and I'll get the bastard again."

Logan released him and Bearchun screamed like a laddie as another arrow flew and pinned his shoulder to the tree.

Then Donnan noticed where the first arrow had landed, right between the man's legs. His bollocks had been pinned to the tree—it was the only explanation for the twisted scream of agony that ripped from Bearchun's gut.

Bearchun's guards began to mutter and chatter amongst themselves, each dropping their weapons as the realization hit them, too.

"His bollocks."

"She pinned him in his sac."

"It must be the Ramsay bitch. She's done it before."

"He can't move. Look at the blood pouring down his legs."

Three men came running up from the back of the castle, arms in the air, weapons left behind, screaming, "We'll bring them to you. They're not in the ground—they're in the cottage in the back. Just don't shoot! Don't shoot my bollocks!"

Gwyneth dropped out of the tree, her bow still in her hand ready to shoot, and said, "Finish him, Logan." She pointed her arrow at one of the men who'd come around from the back and said, "Take me to the lassies."

Molly dropped out of the other tree.

Logan threw a fist into Bearchun's face and said, "Too late, Gwynie. He's already gone."

The squeal of two little lassies reached Donnan's ears as the girls tore around the side of the curtain wall, headed straight for Gwyneth and Molly.

Bethia squeezed Donnan's hand and said, "My sister." He gave her a nod and urged her to join the group now standing in front of the gates, crying and laughing.

Gavin whistled as he jumped down from his tree, causing a stampede of horse's hoofs to thunder across the land.

"Mama, do not cry. We're much bigger now," Brigid said. "'Twas not so scary this time."

"We knew you and Uncle Logan would come for us," Jennet said. "Where's Bethia?"

Tears misted Donnan's eyes as he watched Bethia hug her sister. He could see the tears rolling down her cheeks, too. They were all alive. Bethia, Jennet, and Brigid appeared to be physically fine. He was sure it would take some time for the wee lassies to overcome the horror of what had happened to them this night, but no more wee lassies would be harmed by Bearchun, and Glenna could no longer ruin him or hurt Bethia.

Jennet noticed the horseman leading the others through the trees and yelled, "Papa!" She ran to her father, who scooped her up and settled her on his lap.

"Well done, Gwyneth," Quade winked at her. "You gave him exactly what he had coming to him. Your reputation stands."

Donnan watched the family's reunion with a happy heart, but as he thought over everything that had transpired, a strange urge possessed him. He snuck past the small gathering and let himself inside the gates, then headed up the stairs and into the great hall.

This was his childhood home.

Once inside, the urge that had brought him here gave way to a deluge of tears. He fell into a chair by a trestle table. His arms dropped onto the wooden surface, his head following suit as sobs wrenched from his gut, onto his clothing, and all over the table.

Tears for his son and his sire intermingled until he could no longer see, his wails echoing through the large chamber. His own wife had killed their wee laddie, smothering the breath from his slight form.

He'd find Shewolf and give her the biggest bone he could find. She'd not only saved Bethia, but she'd given him the opportunity to live again.

In a soft voice only he could hear, he whispered, "You were right, Papa. Forgive me for my foolishness. But now I've found a lass whom I'm certain would meet your approval."

He lifted his head and brought his gaze around the chamber he knew so well, wondering how his sister and his sire's servants were. The hall was still decorated beautifully, tapestries and well-carved furniture in front of the hearth with thick cushions everywhere. His thoughts vanished when the door opened and Bethia stepped inside with her sire and her uncle.

Bethia rushed to his side and placed a hand on his one shoulder, checking his other shoulder, the wounded one, before she spoke. "Are you all right? Forgive us for intruding, but I told my sire and uncle about Glenna and what she said. Donnan, I'm so sorry for all of the sorrow you have borne, but you did not kill your son. I hope you take some comfort from that. She was an evil woman."

He pushed back from the table and stepped away from it, his shoulders squared, wiping the tears from his eyes before he spoke. He wrapped his uninjured arm around Bethia's shoulder and kissed her forehead before he turned to face the Ramsay brothers. "My laird...never mind. Just a moment." He turned his attention back to Bethia. "Bethia Ramsay, I formally declare my love for you." He paused to clear his throat. "Your compassion, your patience, and your heart inspire me and others every day. The wee ones love you, the animals would follow you forever, and your family loves you so much that they'd tear apart an army to protect you." He glanced over at Logan, who was actually smiling...slightly. "I know I could not possibly prove myself worthy of being your husband, but I'd welcome the honor and pleasure of having you by my side for the rest of my life." He removed his hand from her shoulder and dropped to one knee in front of her. "And I know my sire would be proud to call you the Countess of Panmure. Bethia, would you do me the honor of becoming my wife?"

Bethia squealed and threw her arms around Donnan. "Aye. I love you, Donnan."

He gave her a chaste kiss once he stood, but then stepped away to address her sire. "My laird, I'd like to ask for your permission and your blessing of this union. I love your daughter with all my heart, and I vow to protect her with my life."

Quade asked, "Shouldn't this question have come to me before my daughter?"

"Nay!" Logan shouted, wide-eyed. "Not unless you wish to incur your daughter's wrath. Donnan and I have endured it once before."

Bethia gave her sire a sheepish grin and nodded.

Before Quade could respond to Donnan's request, the big man pivoted to face Logan. "And I would also like to ask your permission as her beloved uncle, as I have seen the evidence of your feelings for your niece, and I pledge to treat her with the honor and respect she so deserves." He reached for Bethia's hand and squeezed it.

"Hellfire, Douglas, you took an arrow intended for the lass," Logan replied, reaching up to rub his eyes. "My heart skipped at least three beats, and I know not if I'd have survived watching it hit its intended target."

"What in the hell did I miss, Logan?" Quade shouted.

"Be glad you missed it. It nearly killed me. Bearchun gave a signal to his archer, and he released an arrow headed straight for her heart. Donnan stepped in front of it," he pointed to his shoulder. "Did that to him."

"Papa? Have you answered his question?" Bethia's hand gripped Donnan's forearm as they awaited her father's answer. "I'll tend his wound in a moment."

Gwyneth's voice came from outside the door. "Hellfire, answer the man, Quade, so the rest of us can come inside!" She opened the door and peeked around the corner, Jennet, Molly, Brigid, and Torrian all stood behind her.

Quade clasped Donnan's elbow and said, "Aye, you have my permission and my undying gratitude for taking the arrow intended for my daughter." He leaned down and kissed Bethia's cheek as the door burst open and several people shouted with joy, rushing in to congratulate the couple.

Donnan leaned over to kiss Bethia's cheek and whispered, "Are you happy, lass?"

Her face radiant and lovelier than ever, she nodded. "Happier than I had thought possible."

☾

The following day, Bethia settled Donnan at the table in the great hall so she could redress his wound. Many of the Ramsay guards had gone home, along with most of her family, but her mother and father had stayed to help her plan the wedding. They'd gone outside so her mother could search for herbs in the forest with her sire's help, one of their favorite pastimes. Her father had an uncanny ability to see certain herbs from his horse.

Donnan said, "Your hand trembles, my sweet, something I've never seen before."

She let a deep sigh out when she finished, setting on the chair next to him. "Do not fear. Your wound is healing nicely. I worry that I may not meet your sister's expectations, that she'll be disappointed in me when she returns from Edinburgh."

"Nay, that will never happen. My sister is kind-hearted, and she was not overly fond of Glenna. She will be verra pleased to meet you."

She returned her tools to her satchel, setting aside the ones that required cleaning. As she worked, she scanned the hall. "Your sire truly did have a fine hand." She ran her hand across the back of the chair in which she sat. "The scrolling is lovely."

A small smile tipped up his lips. "At first, he kept his talent hidden, believing 'twas beneath his station to craft such treasures, but as he grew older and found I shared his interests, the desire to create blossomed in him again. I'll be forever grateful to him for that."

She took his hand in hers. "Mayhap you should forgive your sire. Relieve your heart of this turmoil between the two of you. Choose to focus on the good memories."

"You are right, and I will do my best to honor his memory, although I have no intention of taking his place."

"And what if we have a son, Donnan? Would you deny him his heritage? Did you consider that before Donnie died?"

"I did, and there were times I wished I had not denounced the title. I'm not sure how I feel about it, but I'll consider your question and give it careful thought." He leaned over and placed a peck on her cheek. "My thanks for your honesty."

The door opened and a man stepped inside, holding the door open for another. A beautiful dark-haired woman followed him into the great hall. She gasped at the sight of Donnan and rushed over to stand in front of him. "Donnan, is it truly you?" She threw her arms around his shoulders. "Dear brother, I have missed you so."

Donnan returned her embrace, but she must have noticed his wound because she ended the hug abruptly. "You're hurt?"

"Nay, do not think on it. Joan, I'd like to introduce you to the woman I plan to marry. This is Bethia Ramsay, and we are to wed within a fortnight."

Joan spun around to greet her. "Welcome to Cairnie Castle, Bethia, and thank you for bringing my brother back to me. I have missed him dearly." The tears misting her kind eyes told Bethia exactly how much she meant those words. Suddenly her fears melted away. This was no cruel or demeaning woman—Joan was just as warm and loving as her brother.

As soon as she introduced them to her husband, Joan tugged Donnan over to the hearth, and they spent the next two hours becoming reacquainted. Their laughter and tears filled the hall, while Bethia and Joan's husband chatted and enjoyed the reunion. When their conversation finally lulled, Joan's husband nodded to her. She made her way to the mantel over the hearth, opened the hinged box atop it, and retrieved a sealed parchment.

She returned to Donnan's side and said, "Papa wrote this when his illness started."

His name was printed in bold letters across the envelope with the words, "The Fourth Earl of Panmure," underneath it.

Bethia glanced at Donnan to gauge his reaction. Emotion flickered across his face as he traced the letters with his finger.

He thanked his sister, then glanced at Bethia. All she could do was nod, encouraging him to open the note. How she hoped this letter would help put an end to the pain he endured whenever he thought of his father. He deserved the chance to recapture the happy memories of his youth.

❦

Donnan turned the letter over and over in his hand.

Joan said, "We're going to head to our chamber. You should read this in private." She sent the servants off with different tasks.

Bethia got up to leave, but he reached for her hand and said, "Nay. Please stay."

She nodded and sat down, folding her hands in her lap.

After much deliberation, he broke the seal of wax and unfolded the parchment, reading it aloud so Bethia could hear it.

Son,

It is with both sorrow and gratitude that I pen this note to you. Sorrow because I know my time is near, gratitude because this new development in my life has forced me to re-evaluate my choices.

I've missed your presence in my life. Your sister and I have both been deeply saddened by your absence. Once I discovered my time was limited, I had my steward gather some information about you.

You have my deepest sympathy for the loss of your son. I'm sorry I did not have the pleasure of seeing you together.

I am not sorry that your relationship with Glenna did not withstand the tragedy you were both forced to endure, but I won't speak any more on that subject.

I wish to tell you how much it has pleased me to hear about your continued interest in building new things. I've heard you've fashioned some wonderful contraptions in your home built of logs.

I'm pleased to hear you've chosen to join the Ramsays. They are good people, and if you stay in good standing with Logan and Quade Ramsay for the rest of your days, I would be proud.

As a dying man and father, I find I have several wishes yet. What do I wish for?

I wish you'd find another woman deserving of your love, one who would return your love and bring you happiness.

I wish I'd been a better man and swallowed my pride, my stubbornness. For that, I apologize.

I wish you would take your rightful place as my heir. It is yours, and it is what your sister wants, and what your dear mother would want.

*I wish you many children, as despite my behavior, you and
your sister have been the two lights of my life.
Above all, I wish you much happiness.*

*With much love,
Your father,
William Douglas
The Third Earl of Panmure*

He folded the letter and returned it to the box on the mantle.
What little remained of the wall he'd built around his heart had
just crumbled.

"What are you thinking?" Bethia asked.

He looked at the woman he adored and reached for her hands,
intertwining his fingers with hers. Her generous heart would want
him to forgive his father, and he had to agree. If he and Bethia had
a son one day, and he and the lad had a bitter argument, he knew
he'd wish for his son's forgiveness. So how could he withhold it
from his own father? It was time to let the bitterness go.

"I'm thinking that if a father truly loved his son, his heart would
be broken if his son chose the wrong woman to marry," he finally
said. "What do you think?"

Bethia stepped close enough for him to see the tears misting her
eyes. Tugging his hands up with hers, she unclasped their fingers
and pressed her palms to his. "I think your sire regretted his actions.
'Tis clear he wished the best for you, and that he did indeed love
you as any father would love his son."

"I cannot disagree with you." He lifted his chin and stared into
her beautiful brown eyes, admiring the sparkling flecks of gold.
How he adored this woman.

How he wished his sire had been given the opportunity to know
her...

"Loving Donnie has changed me. I find I'm more open to forgiveness."

"Aye, your son helped you grow into a more mature man who
is able to give more of himself, and I am grateful to have met you
when I did."

"I know this is something I have no right to ask, but will you promise to never leave me? I don't know what I'd do without you."

Bethia pushed their hands aside and leaned in close, wrapping her arms around his neck. "I promise. And do you know what many in my family say?"

"Nay, please do share," he whispered as he kissed her cheek, breathing in her wonderful scent.

"That you will see your sire again one day. Does that ease your mind?"

"Aye, but not for the reason you think."

She tipped her head, a question in her gaze.

"Because I would like to introduce you to him, and if your beliefs are true, then I'll have that opportunity someday."

CHAPTER TWENTY-FOUR

A SENNIGHT PASSED AND BETHIA'S STOMACH would not calm down, no matter how much she told herself Donnan loved her for who she was inside. He'd told her many times how beautiful he found her, but she'd never truly *felt* beautiful. Her cousin, Molly, had sought her out for a talk, and she'd promised Bethia that her perception of herself would change after marriage. When pushed for an answer, Molly had simply said that love changed everything. But while Donnan's love had changed much in her life, Bethia often felt lacking. How she hoped her wedding day would change that...

They had agreed to marry in Edinburgh as the Earl of Panmure should, and she would carry the title of countess, but they would live in the home Donnan had built, not far from her parents, and not far from the animals she treated for the clan. Joan and her husband would live in the castle, but they would visit with them often.

In another sennight, Bethia would become Donnan's wife, the Countess of Panmure. The trepidation she felt over marrying in Edinburgh in front of droves of people had almost been too much for her, especially since she had not yet seen the dress she was to wear.

Donnan's sister, Joan, whom she adored, had told Donnan about the wedding gown their mother had ordered many, many years ago, soon before her death. She'd announced it was to be for Donnan's future wife. Her maid had passed the message on and kept the gown hidden away. The former earl had refused to bring it out for Glenna.

This was a gown fit for a countess, made with jewels and lace, beads and silk, with all the trimmings. How Bethia hoped the gown had not been made for some petite lass.

Donnan had arranged for the seamstress to come to Cairnie Castle to assist with the adjustment of the gown. He had offered his chamber for the event because it was the only one large enough to hold them all as well as the gown. Her mother and all the sisters and cousins had begged to stay in the countess's dressing room, anxious to see Bethia in her gown, but she had sent the rest of the family downstairs to wait. Many of them had arrived the previous eve to share this special occasion with her. Donnan's sister, the seamstress, the maids who were helping her with the dress, and Bethia's mother would be the only ones in the room when she tried it on the first time. Brenna seemed to feel almost as anxious as she did.

The seamstress who'd made the gown had taken one look at Bethia and smiled, though that smile could mean any number of things. Joan and the maids and seamstress had gone off to fetch the gown, and Bethia stood in the middle of the chamber on a pedestal, already dressed in a silk chemise and beaded slippers.

The giggling chatter of her family carried up the stairs. She heard Aunt Gwyneth and Aunt Avelina, along with her sisters, Lily and Jennet. Her cousins were having a fantastic time. Sorcha, Brigid, Molly, and Maggie were all there, along with several of her Grant cousins—Kyla, Elizabeth, Gracie, and Elyse.

She prayed she would not be embarrassed in front of everyone she loved.

Her mother, as if reading her thoughts, said, "Bethia, you will be beautiful even if the gown is not your color."

Joan came into the room from the next chamber, gave her shoulders a squeeze, and said, "Are you ready? They're bringing it in now. My mother—" she teared up, "—must have had a premonition that my dear brother would meet you. The gown is perfect."

She held the door open and the maids carried it in.

The entire gown was ivory silk, a brilliant shade that was a glorious contrast to Bethia's dark hair. The lace at the top of the gown was a rich gold brocade, but the most striking feature was the golden belt encrusted with jewels that would cinch her waist.

It was so beautiful that her eyes misted. She knew it would never fit.

As they dropped the gown over her head and shoulders, she ducked into it. The folds fell around her, gold threading visible as the fabric floated down over her hips.

She held her breath, waiting in expectation. She'd been through this so many times before. The seamstress would do the usual tugging on the ribbons in the back, tugging and tugging until Bethia wished to cry from embarrassment.

Nothing beautiful ever fit her.

Except this time it did.

Cecily said, "Oh my. Your mother would be so pleased, Joan. 'Tis a perfect fit."

Bethia stared wide-eyed at her mother, who looked like she was about to burst into tears. "Mama?" She didn't know what to make of her mother's expression. "What do you think?"

Joan handed Cecily the belt and the maids tied it around her waist, looping the ends in the back.

"This fits, too," Cecily added. "Your mother always amazed me, Joan. How did she know this would be a perfect fit for Donnan's true wife?"

Everyone in the chamber stood back to admire the gown. Bethia's mother started to cry, Joan and Cecily beamed, and then something miraculous happened.

Bethia looked down at the gown and suddenly felt beautiful.

Cecily played with her hair until it fell in beautiful waves down her back. "Oh, I think we should intertwine golden ribbons with the waves in her glorious hair the day of the ceremony. Don't you agree, Joan?"

Joan smiled and said, "You will make a beautiful bride and a lovely countess."

Her mother couldn't say a word at first—she was choking back her tears. When she was able to manage, she whispered, "Stunning, absolutely stunning. The full skirt hides your hips and your waist looks so small with that belt. It's just…"

"Come," Joan said. "I'll carry your train and you can go downstairs and show your family. I made sure the men are gone, though I'm not sure where Donnan disappeared to. He had a plan. I could tell by the light in his eyes. Bethia, you know not how it pleases me to have my brother back again…and whole. That…that woman had torn apart our family. Many thanks to you, my dear."

They stepped into the passageway, her cousins' voices and laughter filling the hall with joy. She swallowed and made her way toward the wide, curved staircase, pausing at the top to gather her strength, but then she reminded herself.

She was beautiful.

She took two steps down the stairs and a hush fell over her family. Not allowing anything to stop her, she continued, thinking about how much she loved Donnan and how happy they would be together.

Her chin lifted as the quiet was broken by squeals of joy. Her cousins heartily agreed with what her mother had told her.

The Countess of Panmure was a beautiful woman.

☾

Donnan had stayed out of sight, wanting to see whether or not Bethia was satisfied with the gown. He knew how sensitive she was about her size, and if the dress made her feel at all uncomfortable, he would have another one made for her. His breath caught in his throat as soon as soon as he saw her in it, and he could tell from the way she floated down the staircase that his mother had made a fine choice. He watched as her family fussed over her, so pleased that she actually felt as beautiful as he found her to be.

Her beauty came from her heart, her soul, and her stunning smile. True, her chestnut hair fell in luscious waves down her back, and the ivory color of the gown accented her coloring perfectly, but the smile that radiated from her not only lit up her face, but everyone else in the hall.

How could they not feel it? The beauty of her kind soul washed over everyone, even wild wolves, to the point where it was impossible not to bask in her joy.

When he was finally able to tear his gaze from his wife-to-be, he found his way up the back staircase. He waited until Bethia made her way back into his chamber and then caught her mother just before she followed her into the chamber, pulling her aside for a quiet conversation.

After he explained what he had in mind, Bethia's mother's eyes misted and she said, "You do love her, Donnan. I'm impressed you've recognized that about her. I'll talk to Quade." She kissed his cheek and headed down the stairs. Once the gown came back out the door for adjustments, he stepped inside the room and said to his sister. "Joan, I'd like to speak to Bethia alone for a moment. Please find her mother and ask her to explain what we just discussed."

He sent everyone out of the chamber and bolted the door behind him, wanting some time alone with his love. Bethia turned around on the pedestal, wrapped in a thick white robe his sister had purchased for her.

"Donnan, is aught wrong? Did you not like the gown on me? I liked it." Her hands shook as she tied the belt around her dressing robe.

"You were beyond beautiful in that gown, my love. My mother truly had a premonition that you would come into my life. But you are more beautiful to me as you stand in front of me now." He moved closer to her. She attempted to step down from the pedestal, but he stopped her. "Please stay. 'Tis where you belong, my love."

The expression in her eyes told him she didn't understand his meaning. "To me, you are above everyone, though I know you don't see it. Allow me to ask you a question and I ask you to be honest with me." He walked around her in a circle, his gaze taking in her beauty before he came up behind her, wrapping his arms around her waist and pulling her close.

While she was on the pedestal, her head was almost on level with his, a closeness he quite liked. He whispered in her ear, "Were you comfortable in that gown?"

Her voice came out barely loud enough for him to hear. "Aye." She tipped her head down, but he lifted her chin back up. "I love it. It makes me feel beautiful, but…"

"But? Do not be ashamed. That gown is beautiful, and 'tis perfect for you, but I can tell this wedding is straining you. I know that because I love you. I think my wife-to-be would be more comfortable with a small ceremony with just her family and mine in attendance than with a large, formal ceremony in front of a crowd. That she would rather not parade down the streets of Edinburgh before marrying in a castle courtyard in front of hundreds of well-wishers. We would dance for hours, be the center of attention for the entire day before we could sneak away in the late hours of the night."

A tear slid down her cheek and he kissed it away. "Am I correct, sweeting?"

She nodded, her hands gripping his around the waist. "I'm so sorry. I know you're the earl and there are certain expectations for you, but I am so unsettled about all this. 'Tis not how I was raised, 'tis so unlike…"

He put a finger to her lips and said, "Shhh… It is done. I was so sure of it that I've already arranged for it to happen. Cecily will finish the gown for you. 'Tis a gift from my mother to you, and I hope you would like to wear it at our wedding, But if not, we can keep it at the castle for you to use on another occasion. The gown will be at your disposal. If you agree, we will marry quietly in two days, and then I will take you to our home in the woods. We'll spend our first night together there. I've already spoken with your mother."

"Oh, Donnan." She spun around and wrapped her arms around his neck, kissing him until they were both breathless. "And until then?" she whispered, her breath and her body as heated as his own.

"You are all mine. I will show you how much I love you without saying another word." He cupped her face and asked, "Do you trust me, lass? I promise not to take your maidenhead until after we marry, but I have much to teach you." His voice came out a bit huskier than he'd expected, but this woman caused a fire in his body unlike any other.

"I trust you."

He said, "Tell me to stop if I discomfit you."

She nodded, the expression of trust on her face humbling him.

He kissed her cheek and untied the belt around her waist, opening her voluptuous body to him since. Sliding his hands underneath the folds of the robe, beneath which her soft, supple skin was completely bare, he caressed her hips and brought his hands up to her breasts, cupping them both, holding them up for his perusal before he dropped his head to one, teasing her nipple with his tongue until he brought it to a taut peak. She shivered at his touch and he smiled, pleased by yet another show of her passion.

He did the same to her other breast, then drew her bud into his mouth, suckling her until she cried out, her arms now gripping his shoulder. "Donnan?"

"Relax, my sweet. Allow me to get to know you." He stepped back and removed his boots, his tunic, and then his plaid. When her eyes widened, he moved back to her. "Aye, give me your hand, and I'll show you the proof of your beauty." He took her proffered hand and set it on his bulging erection. "This is how much I love you. You are perfect to me, and I've never desired a woman more." She wrapped her fingers around him gingerly and he groaned, closing his eyes. "Not yet, sweet one. 'Tis your turn."

She dropped her hands and he returned his attention to her large breasts, suckling them until she cried out. His hands dipped lower, down her sides and across her belly until they reached the vee in her legs. Caressing her nub, he encouraged her to spread her legs, and she did as he'd hoped, her hands returning to his shoulders.

Pleased to see how slick she was, he followed his finger with his tongue until he knelt in front of her. Then he flicked his tongue over her pleasure spot until she cried his name.

"Donnan!"

"Aye, 'tis number one."

He took the tiny bud in his mouth and suckled her, his finger moving inside her, building her need. He wished to show her how wonderful it would be between them. Their anticipation would build until they were alone together once more.

"Donnan! My knees are buckling. Please, Donnan. I know not what to do."

"That's number two and three, though not quite a scream." She gave him a puzzled look amidst her haze of desire, so he stood and reached for her hand, helping her down from the pedestal and onto the bed behind her. Once he had her in the perfect position, he trailed her body with his fingertips, watching the desire and need flush her face.

"Donnan…"

He continued with his caresses until she squirmed beneath his attentions. He returned his lips to the juncture of her thighs, lavishing her mound in an effort to bring her to completion. He licked and suckled, teasing and taunting until she held her breath, just what he'd hoped for. He plunged his finger inside her heat, careful not to go too far, and continued to do so until she crashed over the edge, calling out his name, and convulsed on his tongue, much to his delight.

When she finished, he kissed a path back up her body and rested his body off to her side, his head in his hand, his elbow supporting it.

"That was wonderful." Her gaze found his and she giggled, a glorious sound. But then it stopped abruptly. "But what about you?" She glanced down at his hardness and quirked her brow. "Tell me what to do. 'Tis only right."

"Nay," he whispered as he kissed her cheek. "You have not screamed my name ten times yet as I pledged you would. But I promise you will in the privacy of our own home."

She laughed and he jumped off the bed, reaching to help her to the side of the bed.

The last thing she asked was, "Do you think Joan will mind if I keep this robe? I rather like it."

CHAPTER TWENTY-FIVE

THAT NIGHT, BETHIA FOUND SHE could not sleep. She moved over to her window and pulled the shutter back, the new contraption she'd never seen, staring up at the crescent moon as she thought about all that had transpired.

Everything had changed at such a rapid pace, and yet it felt like everything had unfolded just as it should. The threat to her family was over, she'd found a wonderful man who adored her, and she was to marry in two days' time—and in the small, private ceremony she'd wanted.

She was so grateful to everyone, but most of all to Donnan. He'd given her so much hope and joy. Love didn't seem like a strong enough word to express her feelings for him. Suddenly, she realized that Molly had been right. When she thought about standing in front of her love with naught on, she felt...beautiful.

How could that be possible?

Suddenly, she knew what she needed to do. Life was just too short to wait for the things you truly wanted. She removed her night rail, donned the plush robe Joan had purchased for her, and cinched the belt around her waist before stepping into the passageway, which she was pleased to find empty.

When she reached his chamber, her boldness took over and she opened his door, stepping inside without waiting for an invitation. Donnan stood in front of his window, but he turned around quickly upon hearing her enter. A small tallow lit the chamber enough for her to see that he was pleased to see her.

"Aye, my love? You seem carried away by your thoughts, just as I've been."

Even in the dark of the night, his handsome looks nearly took her breath away. His beard had grown in enough to look a bit scruffy, but she liked it.

"I promise to trim my beard before we marry." He gazed at her, his eyes widening when she opened her robe, dropping it to the floor as she crossed the space between them.

"I love you however you decide to wear your beard."

"Do you now?" When she was close enough, he dropped his plaid to the floor, the only piece of clothing he had on, and tugged her close, wrapping his arms around her. "You must want more of what you enjoyed earlier. I'd be happy to pleasure you again, sweeting."

His words brought her back to the pleasure he'd given her earlier, to the feeling of his lips on her, laving, licking, suckling her as though she were the finest of treasures. Desire spread through her, but she also felt the need to experience and taste him as he'd tasted her....everywhere.

"I want to know you the way you know me." She caught the surprise in his gaze and decided she'd only begun to understand what the joy of lovemaking could bring to their relationship.

She stood back, watching his erection grow until it jutted proudly in her direction. "I want it all, Donnan. I want you now. I've waited too long for you to come into my life to wait another day. Make love to me." Before he could deny her, she reached for his penis, wrapping her hand around him gently, enjoying the velvety surface and reveling in his response to her touch. Pleased with this new power he'd given her, she moved closer, allowing her nipples to touch the coarse hairs of his chest. She found the sensation quite erotic, rubbing against his skin until her nipples peaked.

"If you do that again, we will finish this." His voice came out in a deep, husky tone that shot straight to her core, spreading a tingling feeling that caused her to lean toward him and scrape her teeth across his nipple.

What had come over her?

He took her hands in his and set her away from him, closing his eyes before he spoke. "Please think about this. Are you sure? Because if I lie in that bed with you, 'twould be sheer torture to stop after I have you in my arms all to myself."

Her thumb traced a path across his lower lip. "I am sure. 'Tis time for us. I must know and feel all of you, Donnan."

"Naught would please me more, but we must be quiet. I care not to awaken all your family. 'Twill be a challenge, but I accept it." With a low growl, he scooped her into his arms and settled her on his bed, shoving the furs aside when he climbed in next to her. "You'll not need anything but me to warm you." The heat of his body enveloped her, speaking to the truth of his words, and she luxuriated in how small she felt next to him. His mouth descended on hers, slanting over her lips so he could caress her more deeply, his tongue teasing hers until she panted with need, her desire now coursing through her with unbridled freedom.

"More, Donnan," she whispered.

His lips trailed a path of kisses down her sensitive neck, across the fine bone beneath to the valley between her breasts. He cupped one breast, bringing the fullness to his mouth, and teased her nipple and the tender underside of the mound until she wished to scream with pleasure.

Deciding it was her turn to taste him, she held his chin up so she could bring her tongue across his beard, raining kisses up to his chin so she could follow his jawline with her tongue, making her way to his ear and then eagerly suckling on his earlobe. Her hands moved from his neck and down his chest, scraping her nails across both nipples until they peaked as hers had done, then wandering down the center of his abdomen until she encountered his hot flesh. She wrapped her hand around him, giving him a light squeeze, surprised to feel a touch of dew at the tip.

"Donnan, more. I need more. Show me, please."

His finger moved to the junction of her thighs, parting her curls until he found her entrance. He instantly groaned. "You are so slick for me, sweeting. I can feel your desire for me."

He caressed her nub and she parted her legs, wanting him inside. She brought the tip of his hardness to her entrance and he gave her the chance to experiment, to push against him where she felt it best. Her hand fell away and her pelvis rose to meet his, loving how his heat seemed to emblazon a path across her folds until she managed to get him inside just a touch.

She moaned as she pushed against him, and he captured her lips in his, but she pulled away. "I don't know what to do now. Please, finish this."

He grabbed her hips and positioned himself at her entrance, coaxing her thighs apart before he plunged inside, breaking her barrier in an instant. She squelched her desire to cry out.

He cupped her face and said, "I'm sorry, but 'tis the only way. 'Twill ease in a few moments." He kissed her forehead. "You are mine forever, lass. 'Tis what it means. I love you and I want you, and only you, forever."

She couldn't stop a tear from escaping from one eye.

"Does it hurt so much?" he whispered. "You cry from the pain, wee one?"

"Nay," she sniffed. "The pain is almost gone. 'Tis the beauty of us that makes me cry tears of joy."

He reached between them and caressed her pleasure spot until she felt the pain ease and her need return.

She moved against him and he slid inside her, then pulled back out. "Nay…stay inside me."

"You are better?"

"Aye."

He thrust inside her and pulled back out again slowly until her need built inside her enough for her to pulse around him. "More."

He moved inside her and she joined him in his rhythm, rocking against him over and over again until her need swelled and pushed her over the edge, her orgasm rocking her insides, her muscles contracting on him until he groaned, pouring his seed into her.

He held her as they both panted, doing their best to calm their breathing. He kissed her lips and rolled to the side of her. "You are not sore?"

"Nay, 'twas most wonderful. Did I please you?"

He sighed and kissed her again. "Aye, you pleased me, more than I even thought possible."

She sighed, resting her head on his shoulder, more pleased than she'd ever been before.

She'd had no idea love could be this wonderful or this all-consuming.

*

Two days later, they married in the middle of the great hall of Cairnie Castle, her mother on one side of her and her sire behind her, and Bethia could not be happier. She kissed her husband with as much exuberance as she dared.

She wore the gown Donnan's mother had created for her and her cousins and siblings stood behind them, along with Joan and her husband, many tears flowing. Once the congratulations ended, Donnan settled his hand around Bethia's waist. He turned to his sister. "I love you, Joan. I know you'll continue to run the castle as well as you always have."

Joan gave both of them a hug and said, "Please promise me you'll visit."

"We will."

Bethia gave each of her cousins a hug and they cheered her on. Lily couldn't stop crying, and Sorcha gave her the biggest squeeze and whispered, "I'm glad you're staying on Ramsay land. I'd miss you too much. We all need you."

Her mother took her by the hand and said, "Say good-bye to everyone. Your husband wishes to take you home this night. We'll follow on the morrow. There are two others waiting to congratulate you outside, and I do hate to keep either of them waiting long."

Puzzled, she waved to everyone while Donnan took the package of food that had been prepared for them. Then she and her new husband followed her mother and father out the door.

Uncle Logan stood outside, brushing one of the horses down. The second guest her mother had spoken of surprised her even more.

Shewolf sat off to the side of the gates.

"Shewolf!" She rushed over to the beast, but did not touch her until the wolf met her eyes. Then she gave the creature a small hug. "Many thanks for saving me, my girl."

Donnan patted the wolf fondly on the head before turning Bethia to face her uncle.

"I know you prefer animals to me. You're my niece. I've known that for years."

She laughed and ran over to throw her arms around her uncle's neck. Her sire watched the two of them with a gleam of fondness in his gaze. "Are you upset that we decided against the big ceremony?"

Uncle Logan chuckled. "Hellfire, nay."

She asked, "Why not? With all your trips to Edinburgh, I thought you'd want me to marry there. I expected you to be more upset than anyone."

"Nay. I wish for you to be true to yourself." He tipped his head to Donnan. "If you wouldn't keep my crown as Queen of the Festival, then how could you possibly wish to be dressed up as a countess and flaunted in front of everyone?"

She couldn't help but smile at her uncle's reasoning.

He was exactly right.

EPILOGUE

TEN MONTHS AFTER HER WEDDING, Bethia sat in her
bed, a smile on her face, watching the man she adored. Her
mother came in and asked, "Is there aught else I can do for you,
Bethia? The birth went beautifully. He's a perfect wee laddie. We
brought meat pies for you that should last a couple of days in that
fancy cold storage your husband built deep in the ground. You still
have fruit. I'll stop by in a few days and help you take a tub bath
if you would like."

Her sire joined her mother, grinning like a fool. "He's a fine
laddie, daughter."

Donnan finally stopped staring at their sweet bairn in the cradle
next to the bed. "Nay, Brenna. I can help her into the tub."

"I wouldn't do it tomorrow. I did have to stitch you in one place,
so I'd let that settle for a few days. You know we'll probably be
back on the morrow." She winked at her daughter and whispered,
"I doubt I'll be able to keep your sire away."

Once they had left, Donnan stared at their son again. "Bethia,
he's perfect. Look how he's sleeping. Your mother said not to leave
too many blankets in the cradle. I like the thick dressing gown she
sewed for him. Mayhap he will not need an extra blanket at night."
He glanced at her, hope in his eyes. "You know how worried my
thoughts will be otherwise. What shall we call him?"

She rested back on the pillows her mother had arranged for her.
"I'm not sure."

"Not Donnie."

"Nay. Not Donnie. But we'll never forget Donnie. I promise.
He's your firstborn. How about Drystan or Drostan? 'Tis not

exactly the same, but 'twould be similar enough to be a tribute to your first son."

"Thank you," he said. He thought for a moment, then replied, "I like that. How about Drystan? It will remind us of Donnie, but he'll be different."

"Aye," she agreed happily.

Still staring at their newly born son, Donnan's brow furrowed when the bairn scrunched his face up and let out a howl, his face turning bright red. "What's wrong with him?"

"Why don't you bring him to me? Mayhap he's hungry."

"Och, Bethia. We forgot to ask your mother about a wet nurse or for some contraption to feed the bairn goat's milk. I can go after her."

She could tell by his expression that he was overwrought. "Donnan, bring him to me. I'll feed him."

He did as she asked, handling the bairn with such care, she had to control her smile. Donnan would be a wonderful father.

She opened her gown and brought the wee babe to her breast. He rooted for a bit, expressing his frustration with his wee fists, but Bethia readjusted him and cooed encouragement to their handsome lad. Once he latched on to her nipple, his fists relaxed and he suckled with pleasure. "Oh, I think he's latched on well."

Donnan continued to stare at her. Tears ran down his cheeks and he turned away, looking for a linen square.

"Husband, I cannot promise he'll live forever, but both of us will do everything in our power to keep this baby alive and well. You believe that, do you not?"

Donnan nodded.

"Why do you cry?"

He reached down to pet Wynda's head, then opened the door to let the dogs outside for a bit. When he came back, tears still slid down his cheek.

"Donnan? Help me understand."

"Glenna never wished to feed Donnie from her breast. She said it didn't work, so we fed him goat's milk. I fed him goat's milk."

"Oh, I'll feed our son. You need not worry about that. I love doing this. It makes me feel close to him. You may sit with us."

"I would like that if you don't mind."

"Of course not."

He moved over to the bed and rested across it, in a perfect position to watch the two of them as Drystan nursed.

After a few moments of observing the mother and child, he whispered, "You worried many days in your life about being beautiful, wife, do you not agree?"

"Aye. I know 'twas foolish of me. As long as I'm beautiful to you, I'll be happy."

He paused, thoughtful about what was in front of him, before he said, "There is nothing more beautiful than you feeding our son. 'Tis the true meaning of beauty to me."

She leaned over and kissed her husband. "I will forever remember that, husband."

THE END

DEAR READERS,

Thank you for reading Bethia's story. This will be the last story in The Highland Clan for a while, but not forever. I will return to it as there are many more stories to tell.

My plan is to pull seven characters from The Highland Clan and give them their own series, as yet untitled. Which ones?

Maggie, Connor, Roddy, Braden, Gavin, Gregor, and David. They will join together for some special excursions…well, that's all I'll say for now, but I promise they will each receive their own story. Stay tuned for this new series in the Grant/Ramsay saga, which will begin in early 2018.

I will also release the next Summerhill novel before the end of the year, Lauren's story.

The last is a super secret story. You'll see.

Happy reading!

Keira Montclair

ABOUT THE AUTHOR

KEIRA MONTCLAIR IS THE PEN name of an author who lives in Florida with her husband. She loves to write fast-paced, emotional romance, especially with children as secondary characters in her stories.

She has worked as a registered nurse in pediatrics and recovery room nursing. Teaching is another of her loves, and she has taught both high school mathematics and practical nursing.

Now she loves to spend her time writing, but there isn't enough time to write everything she wants! Her Highlander Clan Grant series, comprising of eight standalone novels, is a reader favorite. Her third series, The Highland Clan, set twenty years after the Clan Grant series, focuses on the Grant/Ramsay descendants. She also has a contemporary series set in The Finger Lakes of Western New York.

Her newest series is The Soulmate Chronicles, historical romance with a touch of paranormal.